The Ancient Ones

by

K. J. Goss

SHIRES PRESS

4869 Main Street
P.O. Box 2200
Manchester Center, VT 05255
www.northshire.com

The Ancient Ones

ISBN Number: 978-0-9997533-2-3

Building Community, One Book at a Time
*A family-owned, independent bookstore in
Manchester Ctr., VT, since 1976 and Saratoga Springs, NY since 2013.
We are committed to excellence in bookselling.
The Northshire Bookstore's mission is to serve as a resource for
information, ideas, and entertainment while honoring the needs of
customers, staff, and community.*

Printed in the United States of America

The Ancient Ones

Chapter 1

The nameless masterpiece before me, sculpted by untamed winds of the desert transforming sandstone into the wild beauty that was now highlighted by the first rays of the red morning sun held me spellbound. I stood in awe of nature at its finest.

I now was here in the desert for research, but was so overpowered by art at its best I almost forgot my initial purpose. My camera was in its case around my neck and that's where it stayed. My eyes and brain were now my operating photo system. I really didn't care that I missed the shot of a lifetime to show others, but was more than satisfied that it was now indelibly etched in my mind. Without realizing it, almost forty minutes passed in my admiration of the magnificence of simple sandstone.

I had always heard of the ever changing colors of the Southwest desert yet until now had never witnessed it. The time slot for my photo research had passed which meant I would have to wait until tomorrow morning. At least I would be better prepared for the shock of nature. All was not lost. I still looked forward to the setting sun to continue my research.

At this time I guess an explanation of my work is in order.

For the last two years I had spent many months in the Yucatan with a team resurrecting a lost Mayan city. My expertise in aerial photo interpretation proved invaluable.

That led to probably the largest find of the century. A whole new city state encompassing a very large area. The research of such a find planted a bug in me. I needed to assess the areas in hope of again finding something lost to history. As much as I loved the jungle of the Yucatan, I felt a change of venue was in order. Hence, here I am in the desert of the American southwest.

It is a known fact that ancient roadways leading away from Pueblo Bonito connect with other outlying communities. These perfectly straight byways leading to these other settlements are no longer visible to the naked eye because of the winds of time over the ever changing topography, but traces are still there nonetheless, hence my continued research.

The extreme low angles of the sun, both at sunrise and sunset will cast shadows, almost imperceptible, which can manifest themselves in all kinds of shapes, including straight lines that can go on for miles which may indicate ancient roadways. Roadways that could lead to yet undiscovered communities, small cities or rural settlements.

As Eric Dexter, my experiences in the Yucatan with lost cities tweaked my curiosity to look for the same things closer to home. Now I was following that urge. I still kept in touch with my Maya friends at the college in Arizona knowing they would be busy for a few years with the lost city they and Frank Thurber had uncovered. I certainly wanted to keep informed about the scroll translations and what light they may or may not throw on the world. Admittedly, a part of me missed the talks with the king through his mind melds, but the burden of his wisdom was now taken up by Mario and Diego and I knew they would share any worldly enlightenment with me.

Back to the matter at hand, the weather forecast was good for the next few days so I decided to wait out the day and catch the setting sun and see if I could detect any straight line shadows. I was at this particular spot because after perusing the latest U.S.G.S.* air photos of the area it seemed like a logical place to start, due to the location of already known early settlements.

I settled back to await the day enjoying the ever changing colors of the desert as the sun moved its magical light across the sandstone sculpture to fade away in the west. I guess I was a bit too relaxed. I found myself startled awake as a furry blue Tarantula scrambled across my shirt. I hurried him on his way with a quick swat of my hand but not before thanking him for being my alarm click. My over relaxed state nearly ruined my whole day by almost causing me to miss the sunset. I was now alert and concentrating on what I was supposed to be doing.

* United States Geological Society

Camera ready, I watched and waited. A bit disappointed, I was about to give up when it happened. A straight line appeared being slowly drawn on the desert floor, faint in some places but a line none the less.

I hurriedly shot as many frames as I could, at the same time making a line of sight direction with my compass to be backed up later with GPS readings. As quickly as the magical line appeared it faded as the sun dropped below the western horizon.

I felt exhilarated but cautioned myself on getting over excited about something that may not be what I wanted it to be. Using a sighting compass I was able to pick out a distant land mark that I could later, with a GPS reading, transfer to my working map. That is if I can get enough info to make a working map.

Unlike the Chaco Canyon area which is full of Anasazi ruins and history I was trying my luck in a totally different location. It was close to the Chaco area but away from the known ruins and landmarks. A lot of people ask me what is it that I look for in aerial photography to identify areas of interest. The answer is difficult. There is no one thing specifically. When viewing air photos stereoscopically, certain features stand out to a trained eye. Believe it or not a gut feel has a lot to do with it also, at least for me anyway. On this particular site I did comparison studies with already known sites and found similar depressions aligned to the cardinal compass points. This led me to being here today.

Darkness was now setting as I gathered my equipment together and packed it away in my rental SUV. Tomorrow would be another very early day, weather permitting.

-Ancient Ones-

Chapter 2

As planned I arrived back at yesterdays location and set up my equipment in the dark. Well not quite dark, there was a three quarter moon casting it's light on the sculptured desert monuments. Again I lost myself in the deserts beauty, so much so that I almost missed the sunrise again. Keeping my eyes on yesterdays alignment I waited anxiously. Suddenly it was there, the shadow line I was anticipating. Offset about twenty five feet it paralleled the line of the night before. My heart was thumping, my mind racing. Could this lead to yet another settlement or fill in a piece of missing history. Like other lost peoples of long ago, the Anasazi or "Ancient Ones" are still behind a cloud of mystery as to their origin, both when and where..

Back to the task at hand. Looking in the opposite direction before I lost the sun, my hopes soared even more when I detected the shadow's continued path behind me. I took my line of sight and GPS readings just as the shadows disappeared as the angle of the sun changed.

Pleased with myself I relaxed and enjoyed the color show unfolding before me. Unfortunately two early mornings in a row caught up with me and I awoke to the scream of an eagle high above me. I felt better even though it interrupted my dream. It seems the Mayan king still invaded my thoughts, or at least my dreams.

I decided to call it a day seeing that it was close to one PM and would give myself the rest of the afternoon to plot my results on my working map and research the resultant directions. Who knows where they will lead or what they will lead to.

Back at my mini-kitchen motel suite my mind drifted to my Mayan friends and the king. To ease this yearning I reached for the phone, dialing Mario's number which only gave me an answering machine. I followed this by pushing the buttons for Diego's office. It felt good hearing his voice. They were still at the college in Arizona planning their expedition in about three weeks. Diego said that both he and Mario had some short contact   with the king but were expecting more lengthy communication back at the lost city. I remembered to remind Diego that the king liked to speak in riddles. He agreed to pass my regards to the king.

Alone with my own thoughts again I pushed myself back to my chosen research. Plotting my finds to date seemed to point in a direction I had not anticipated. I then planned for another early start the next day hoping the sun would cooperate. I dozed off for the night to some stupid movie on the tele. At least I didn't miss anything.

Chapter 3

No matter how many times I see the sunrise in the desert I never tire of it's magnificence. I had set up my equipment early to allow myself a quick glance before paying attention to my purpose of being there. Not surprised but still thrilled, my straight line shadows appeared again though almost indistinguishable. I made the usual recordings and sightings then proceeded to relax for the day awaiting the low angle sunset and more photography. I dug out my special area map which I had marked all the known ruins I could identify through my previous research. Studies from other people already identified some fifteen hundred plus miles of roadways between early occupied sites especially outgoing from Pueblo Bonito. There does not seem to be anything built after eleven hundred forty. I then realized I had better recheck my own research to ascertain whether or not I'm only rediscovering a known road. That would have to wait for tonight though back at the motel room. I'll just keep my fingers crossed that I am onto something new.

I stretched out in the shadow of an overhang as I so often did in the jungle of the Yucatan though I did miss the choir of the jungle with its soothing music.

My blue tarantula friend was my alarm clock again, otherwise I would have missed the sunset. I know most people have heard of tarantulas, but few have ever seen one. For the uninitiated to the Southwest desert, particularly the four corners area, the creatures of nature come rather large. Picture, if you will, a body size of a coffee cup opening, you know three to five inches across. If you take into consideration the leg extensions you are looking at roughly an eleven inch plus or minus overall size. Believe it or not these hairy, scary things actually can be quite beautiful showing off their various colors. My particular friend here was sporting a cobalt blue coat that was very striking.

Camera and compass ready, I was not disappointed. My straight line showed itself, broken though it was it went on forever. It only

lasted for seconds, nevertheless I managed to record it.

Relaxing in my temporary home away from home I chose not to make it an early morning for the next few days. I wanted to seriously and accurately plot and track this new find. Right now I could only wish to have the same success I had with the lost city in the Yucatan. I gave myself the luxury of a dinner out and when I returned I further spoiled myself with a cognac as I studied the maps in front of me.

On a clear overlay I transferred my new, or at least I hoped it was new, roadway to match scale with the known ruin plots. I plotted my measurements as accurately as I could and when I finished I stared at my map dumbfounded. I could not believe what I was seeing. My plot of what I hoped was a roadway was in the middle of nowhere. No ruin sites, no pueblo centers, no intersects with other roads, old or new, nothing. Just one straight line avoiding the magnificent sandstone sculptures. Then who knows what they looked like a thousand plus years ago. Neither the start or finish made sense. There was nothing to connect within fifty miles at either end. I sat there for who knows how long just staring at the map, my mind a total blank. This is where I could have used the king for some input, riddles or not. Then again this is not the Yucatan. Pushing myself alert I realized I may be looking at something new. The peoples of the past, such as the Anasazi or perhaps even earlier ancestors usually built everything aligned with the cardinal compass points. This new plot of mine definitely was not the case or my plot was just totally out to lunch. As I further scanned my map it dawned on me that over the course of three thousand years, magnetic and true North could have changed due to the earth's orbit and or wobble. If this was the case perhaps my plot is not wrong.

Clearing my head for a moment and just looking out the window thinking of nothing, a thought exploded like a light bulb. Possibly this "roadway" had nothing to do with the cardinal points. Maybe it was pointing to something special. I sat down at the table again muttering aloud; "There goes my wild imagination again." I think perhaps I spent too much time in the Yucatan listening to the king. It seems now I want everything to be special and just for me. Talk about being spoiled.

I decided to put everything on hold for now until I returned to the desert. I put my map and overlays away and decided it was bedtime. Oh how I missed my hammock and jungle music.

Chapter 4

It was mid morning by the time I started my drive back to the desert. The only map I brought with me today was the general area map showing Ancient Ruins spread over the four corners region. Arriving at the beginning of my new roadway I scanned three hundred sixty degrees and aligned the nearest ancient sites with my plot. This would yet again provide me with another overlay. Securing my various readings I moved on to the other end of my new road, at least still hoping it was a road. My road as it turned out was just over two miles long. Repeating my three hundred sixty scan and recording results left me with absolutely nothing. I still could find no relationship of the one thing to another.

Feeling disappointed and let down I headed back to the start. At about the halfway point, and still feeling sorry for myself, I flopped down on the desert floor, my mind sort of blank. I had set myself up for this letdown. After all Archeologists had been combing the four corners area for some two hundred years, why should I think I was someone special to locate something no one else could find..

It was getting late and the sun would disappear soon, so rather dejectedly I decided to head for the motel. At that point my ears detected the rustle of some sand. Turning in the direction of the disturbance I spied a side winder curving his way down a small slope. I watched it for a few seconds as it wiggled its way across a dark line onto another slope. *"Dark line?"* I thought. There are no dark lines in the desert. Readjusting my gaze from the snake to the dark line, it was gone. I then realized the sun was setting and what I probably saw was a low angle shadow from the sun as in the roadway I already plotted. I could feel my heart pounding in my chest. I instantly took a GPS reading. I could do little else, as the sun was now too close to the horizon. Elated as I was, I was also saddened by the fact that I would now have to wait till tomorrow to do any further sightings.

My spirits renewed I happily returned to the motel and dinner.

The next morning I had arrived and already set up my camera and GPS at yesterday's discovery. I waited impatiently for the sun disc not taking my eyes from my target site. Finally there it was. My dark line shadow. It was not as distinct as the original lines I plotted but it was there nonetheless. It looked to be exactly ninety degrees to my original lines. As slow as the sun moved it was fast enough to deny me the opposite direction, if there were lines in that direction. I would just have to wait for sunset. Oh well, back to the motel, lunch and a nap.

Surprisingly the nap did not come easily. I could not shut my mind off. Was this really a new causeway or just wishful thinking? If it was a road why in the middle of nowhere ? If not a road, what was it ? And why ?

Patience ,Eric, patience, the truth will be known soon enough. *"Now I'm beginning to sound like the king."* I thought. I eventually did doze off and was awakened by some ones car alarm, and of course it was dark.. I missed the sunset totally though I was not really disappointed. I arranged better planning for the next day. Catch the sunrise then spend the rest of the day on a more thorough inspection of the roadway, particularly this half way point. I would do the more serious plotting this evening. I was counting on some sort of relationship between the known ruins and my newly discovered roadway.

A quick supper break and finishing what plotting I could do and I hit the bed still exhausted.

Chapter 5

My early morning sun vigil was a bit of a disappointment. The extended line shadows only went about fifty feet either way from the main causeway. This of course presented many new questions. Perhaps more disappointment than questions. Once shadows vanished I sat back on the desert floor to try and figure what this was all about. It just didn't make sense that the Ancient Ones would start to layout a road equidistant in both directions and then just give up. There must be a reason for this. Questions many, answers none. *"Where is the king when you need him ?"* I asked myself.

I wandered to the apparent end of this short roadway but nothing was obvious. "Of course not." I answered myself out loud, "We're talking hundreds or even thousands of years of shifting and windblown sands. What did you expect to find ?   A door to all the answers ?"

I reversed directions and found exactly the same thing; absolutely nothing. I chose not to wait for sunset and returned to the motel. On the way back I noticed a local utility worker using a metal detector to locate pipes or something.

"**M**aybe that's what I need." I said aloud. "Either that or some kind of a sonar sounding machine to check for anomalies underground. Of course there is always Lidar,∗ but that laser probe equipment can get expensive.   There's also the expense of renting the helicopter for the overflight. At least with the sonar stuff you push or pull it over the ground like a lawn mower. That's really way over my budget of no dollars, besides where do I find it out here in the middle of nowhere. Who am I kidding, look at me trying to be an expert on something I know nothing of. A little success in the Yucatan does not make me qualified to study in the desert. At least in the jungle I could rely on my expertise in Aerial Photo interpretation. I sat back staring at nothing for how long I don't know when suddenly my brain started working again.

∗ Lidar (Light Detection and Ranging) Lasar to probe landscapes.

"**W**ait a minute." I yelled out loud, "Maybe I just answered my own question. My expertise is in photographic mapping and photo interpretation. I was successful in the Yucatan; why not use it here."

I did have with me the latest air photo overflight of the area and the most recent USGS topographic maps. All I had to do was figure out what bag I packed them in. With a sudden renewed spirit I started going through the various suitcases. Without much difficulty I located the neatly identified envelopes holding my precious livelihood. Finding the appropriate photo's and topo's of my area of concern I cleared a space on the table and went to work.. Getting back to the love of my life was a good feeling and I found myself humming an unidentified tune. Wanting something a little more substantial than my own off key sounds, I switched on the radio, and found the local classical music station, the perfect background for my work.

Exactly pinpointing my study area by recorded coordinates, I let my eyes do their thing matching air photo anomalies with the contours. At first I didn't believe what I was seeing, but after double and triple checking I was convinced that I had found something, at least a very good possibility of something. I relaxed for a short while to give my eyes and mind a break. I even walked away from my maps.

I grabbed a cold brew from the fridge and took my time drinking the first half forcing myself to stay away from the maps. Finally giving in to my inner cravings I returned to the maps. My findings had not changed. It seems I was successful once again using my training of years ago. There was definitely something strange at my roads to a nowhere intersection. My interpretation of the contours from the topo map with the barely visual anomalies of the air photos showed a definitive shape at the intersection. The East and West sides matched each other but were different from the North and South sides which also matched each other. My wishful thinking told me this had to be man made. *"There I go again, letting my imagination rule my common sense."*

Now came the task of how to prove my wishful thinking. I can't just start digging. This is not my land. This is public land or Navajo Nation land. I will need permission but from whom? I suddenly had the down in the dumps feeling again. I decided then and there not to let it get me too down. I would return to my crossroads in the morning for some physical ground research. Doing it the hard way may turn up some clues. You know down on my hands and knees and using my eyes to research. I checked my watch, it was too late to call Mario or Diego now, but that was certainly on my list for tomorrow. Perhaps they would have some helpful hints. I left everything spread out on the table, killed the light and fell into bed and clicked on the TV remote at the same time.

Chapter 6

I awoke to some children's early show trying to sell me some much too sweet breakfast cereal. Since it was already way past sunrise I decided not to go to the desert today. Perhaps a trip to the local library would help keep me grounded, but first a few phone calls. I waited until after nine to make sure Mario and Diego would be in their offices at the college hoping at the same time they had not already taken off for the Yucatan.

I was in luck, Mario answered on the second ring. He sounded genuinely pleased to hear from me. He filled me in with the archeologist information on the scrolls and what they were planning for this seasons expedition. There was a great temptation to want to join them but just as strong was the desire to stay where I was and study things closer to home. I briefly reviewed my present situation with Mario but he could not offer any suggestions though he did say Diego could probably assist me more in that area. I let it go with that and we further discussed this year's trip to the lost city. I didn't mean to be rude but finally cut Mario short and at last he hung up with my promise to call again before they left the States. I was anxious to talk to Diego; we barely disconnected when I found my finger already pushing the buttons for Diego's number. He answered on the first ring as if he was expecting me to call. I reiterated what I told Mario and was interrupted with some good news.

"That's easy, I know I can help. A very good friend of mine I went to school with is a Navaho and lives and works in that area. He is an archeologist slash anthropologist and is furthering the study of his own people. Give me a day or so, I'll see what I can do for you."

I was elated and thanked Diego profusely. I was still on a high after we hung up and decided to go back to the desert anyhow. I filled the rest of my day with trivial things that I normally would not have bothered with, but today they all seemed important to me. The day passed quickly so about mid afternoon I felt a rest was earned , so I sat back to enjoy the beauty of the desert. As I lost myself in the muted color scheme that washed over the sandstone sentinels I had a visitor. My friendly blue tarantula was slowly approaching. This may sound ridiculous but I gave it a friendly greeting while reaching for my camera.   Since he helped me a few days ago I felt it appropriate to make him a permanent part of my research. I swear he knew what I was doing as I captured him from all angles. When I finally put the camera down he slowly sauntered away in the direction he came from. I laughed to myself and thanked him out loud.

The sun was quickly nearing its days travel end as I packed up and headed for the motel.

Driving back I reflected on my blue friend again. Did he really know what I was doing ? I think I was actually looking forward to seeing him again.

Chapter 7

The next day I sort of gave myself the day off. I slept in, had a long and lazy breakfast then made my way to the local library, that is if you want to call forty minutes driving local. I found nothing new in the stacks, nothing, that is that I had not already come across in my past readings. Disappointed by the lack of anything new I drove out to the desert again, not for further research but for strictly selfish photographic opportunities. The ever changing color just screamed to be captured.

As always, all good things have an end. The colored beauty of the desert was now mine forever. I must have made close to a hundred exposures of things most people will never see. More than pleased with myself I pointed the car in the direction of the Motel with a lookout for a nice restaurant on the way.

A perfect day I thought as I turned the key in my Suite door. I was met with a blinking light on the telephone cradle.   I checked the message only to find the perfect ending to my already perfect day. It was my Native American contact that Diego spoke of. It wasn't that late so I returned the call and spoke with Dan Harper, a.k.a. Lone Buffalo. He greeted my proposal with much enthusiasm indicating this sort of thing fits in well with his own studies. It was agreed he would meet me here at the motel at nine the next morning.

I had not been this excited in a long time, so I treated myself to a glass of wine and tucked myself in bed.

Up early, showered and dressed and ready by eight o'clock, I made a large pot of coffee planning on sharing it with Lone Buffalo. To pass the rest of my waiting time I prepared myself a light breakfast. Time was now creeping because I was so anxious.

The knock at the door startled me, I must have dozed for a few minutes while waiting. I opened the door to a man in his early thirties, as was Diego, a darkened complexion and neck length dark hair. His eyes showed both warmth and intelligence, overall a rather good looking young man.

"Eric Dexter ?" he inquired.

I held out my hand as I answered in return;

"Dan Harper ?"

We jointly broke into smiles as he clasped my hand firmly.

"Please come in." I said and ushered him to the only soft easy chair in the room. "Coffee ?"

"Sure." he accepted and continued right into business. "I understand you're doing research in my back yard."

At first I was alarmed but saw a big grin spread across his face. I answered more relaxed;

"I was trying to trace ancient roadways that crossed this desert who knows how many years ago and I think I found something, but I'm not sure. Before I go digging where I'm not supposed to I thought I might get some proper information as to how to go about it. That's where our mutual friend, Diego comes in."

"Yes, he briefly outlined your relationship with him and he thinks the world of you. He said you're someone exceptionally special."

I could feel myself go red with embarrassment.

"I fear he goes a bit overboard with his judgement of me, and yes we have a great relationship. I've never seen an artist like him."

"Yeah, he sure is a natural. He's one of the lucky one's who had that talent since birth." Dan replied. "Let's get back to your situation. From what Diego has told me I think I can definitely help. I have all the necessary connections and in addition since I am a Native I can pretty much do as I want, within reason of course. So if we do this jointly I think we can get pretty much of what you want."

I really wanted to jump up and dance around. I was so happy, But better judgement prevailed and I thanked him showing my excitement.

I mentioned to him I had no secrets and brought him to the table where all my plot maps were. He seemed impressed by my thoroughness. I fully explained my work to date. He studied my plots in detail and smiling finally spoke.

"You may be on to something Eric."

I felt my heart go thump.

"The pursuit of my peoples history over these many years

has led of course to the known ruins you have already plotted. There are many others which are only now being excavated, yet I personally feel that there is something missing. We have a living culture, large settlements, trade with other nation's and far away places. Ideas were exchanged. Even our farms were successful until the drought came.

There appear to be pieces missing between today and a few hundred to a possible few thousand years ago." Dan Harper paused at this point then hesitantly continued, "Listen to me, you would think I was back in a classroom teaching again. Forgive me for going on so."

"No need for that." I answered. "I find it fascinating to learn as much as I can about the things I'm investigating. Go back to what you were saying about me being on to something."

"Oh yeah that." Dan replied. "Your specific area of interest, I want to go there with you. I have been over that place many times myself before and would always get this strange feeling. I have no idea what it means, if anything at all, but it's like I'm always drawn to it. I know what you mean."

I picked up on his theme. "I get weird sensations also every time I cross that spot. How busy is your schedule, perhaps we could look the area over together.

"No time like the present." Dan said smiling. "I cleared my schedule for a few days after I spoke to you on the phone."

"That's great." I almost shouted. "Let me grab some equipment and we're on our way."

Chapter 8

The drive to the desert seemed to go faster than usual I thought but I realized having someone to chat with over common interests does make time fly.

Arriving just before noon the area in question appeared stark and bright. Again just another twist of nature with her color scheme. We both stood mesmerized taking in the real life painting surrounding us. Dan finally broke our mutual silence.

"I never cease to be amazed by the desert, no matter how many times I see its different aspects, and I was born and raised here yet it never gets old.

Smiling I agreed with him and broke the magic by unrolling my plot map. Without looking at my map Lone Buffalo walked to a spot he said gave him the strongest pull. Following my GPS I again became excited. Dan had walked to the exact center of my plotted area. I mentioned this to him and he broke out in a big grin.

"You don't know how good that makes me feel. It's like the confirmation of the feeling I've been waiting for. Now my friend, maybe together we can satisfy this unknown calling." We moved closer to each other hands extended to a warm firm hand shake wishing success to each other.

"Enough with the mushy stuff, Where do we start ?"

I further explained to Dan how I achieved my straight line plots, then off handedly suggested some sort of ground sonar apparatus. I was just ready to poo - poo the idea because of the expense beyond my pocket when I saw a smile cross his face.

"Now my friend that is where I come in. The archeological group I work with has just such a machine which I myself have used before. I'm sure I can get hold of it. How about tomorrow ?"

I could not speak, and if I did I didn't know what to say. Again it was like a dream come true. We spent the next few hours combing

our selected section of desert for any sign of anything out of the ordinary. Nothing was obvious. Becoming serious for the moment I had to ask;

"**W**hat if we do record anomalies underground, how do we go about getting permission to excavate ?"

"**T**here again my friend is where I come in. My position and research group have all the credentials and paperwork we need, and remember this is my homeland which gives me certain privileges. I think we can accomplish this."

"**T**his is as good as being with the king." I volunteered.

Dan looked at me with a cloud of confusion covering his face.

"**T**he king ?" he asked.

"**I**'ll fill you in on the way back to the motel."

We cleaned up the few things we had and walked to the car. Once happily on the road I outlined my story of the king. The shortened version of course. I did not want to burden Dan with two years of detail. "A quick synopsis," I stated. "When we first entered the Pyramid tomb we saw a mummified body which appeared to be someone special. Two days later our mummy was up and walking around. It seems the early Maya developed a process of suspended animation. The fresh air from opening the tomb acted as the resuscitation to start the life process again. We co-existed for a while each learning from the other although it was easy to see the king, as we called him, had a far more superior intellect than we. He chose me to communicate with by mental telepathy. It was quite enlightening and most helpful. He did die naturally after a short while but to my surprise the mental conversations continued and probably still would if I stayed in the Yucatan. It was agreed when I left the king would choose other members of our team to further this method of communication. As a matter of fact our mutual friend Diego is one of them. If for any reason you ever wanted to know more, we all kept journals of our experiences and historical finds. You are more than welcome to read mine. Knowing Diego you could probably have access to his also. And that's the king I was referring to."

"**D**iego mentioned something about a mummified Mayan king. I did not pay attention to the whole story. Dan offered. "You're right though he would come in handy about now."

Back at my motel I parted company with Dan, or Lone Buffalo, who promised to be back early the next day with the necessary equipment to continue our probe into the mysteries of the desert.

Alone again with my maps, I tried once more to make better sense of my plots such as why did the "road" start and end in the middle of nowhere ? Why also were the two lengths the same and cross exactly in the middle of each other? This left me with a center with arms exactly one half mile long extending in direction just off the major cardinal points of the compass. No matter how I viewed my work It revealed nothing to me. It appeared that the desert did not want to give up its secret.

Chapter 9

I awoke filled with anticipation of the coming day. MY spirits soared with yesterdays revelations from Lone Buffalo. I found myself thinking of Dan as I would the king, some one special that had access to a knowledge unknown to me. A proper and thorough breakfast I felt was in order. Checking the clock I found I had adequate time for just such a thing and I savored every morsel.

I just finished checking my equipment and backpack when I heard Dan's knock at the door.

Upon opening the door I could see over his shoulder a green pickup truck with a drag over the earth: the Sonar Sounding machine. I felt like screaming like a child yet forced myself to remain adult and professional.

"How's that for a toy." Dan said through a huge smile. "Now maybe we can answer some of your questions or more correctly some of both of our questions."

"I'm just about ready. Let me just kill these lights and we're on our way."

We unloaded the machine and double checked that everything was in working order, loaded the plotting paper, ascertaining all the electronics were functioning.

We chose the south end to start and even starting about fifty feet before my roadway plot. We wished each other luck and started our first run. It was slow and tedious pulling this sled across the desert sand and gravel. We took turns pulling and pushing, attempting to keep it as smooth as possible.

Checking the electronic print out proved disappointing but we forged on. After approximately one thousand feet the plotter began registering a different signal. An anomaly underground and not very deep. With renewed hope we increased our effort to make our scans as even as feasible. The further we went the more intricate was the printing of the plotter. We were both almost giddy now with thoughts of discovery flooding our heads. Nevertheless we continued our unified effort aiming for accuracy.

It took the better part of an hour and then some to reach the halfway point, all the time recording a slight change in plot. This slight change meant nothing to us at the moment except that there was some sort of disturbance below ground. We both knew it could be good, bad or nothing. Dan and I rested for a few minutes to catch our breath before completing the next mile of dragging the sledge holding the scanning equipment. Our rest was short lived for we were both anxious to resume our endeavors hoping for the results we desired. Our push pull efforts increased when we realized the terrain took a slight uphill bent. Even this did not deter our determination. Another hour of sweat brought us to the end of my roadway outline. Dan and I were equally tired but were determined to forge on. We moved the sled over about four feet and made the return journey knowing this overlapping imagery we were recording would net us some positive results. The second run back to our start went so smoothly that we agreed on a third scan. After a short, much needed rest we moved another four feet and repeated the two mile run. More than pleased with ourselves we went for the fouth run. We had to go back toward the car anyway so why not make it productive.

The last run ate up almost an hour and a half by the time we dismantled the equipment. We were both weary from our efforts but remained stimulated about the upcoming results. We rested with some cool water after re-packing the vehicle.

Dan suddenly showed an alarmed look.

"Don't move Eric. There's a tarantula nearing your leg, I think I can swat it away if you stay still."

I looked down only to see my blue friend bypassing me as if I were not there.

"Leave him be Dan, that's my friend. More like my good luck charm."

Dan appeared puzzled so I explained my previous encounter with Mr. Blue. You could tell he thought I was half crazy but accepted my explanation with a smile.

"I've heard of many good luck charms before but never a tarantula."

We both watched as it nonchalantly went on it's way.

Convinced that we were rested we climbed into the vehicle and returned to my motel.

I grabbed us each a cold one and together we set up the post processing equipment. I found some chips and nuts to nibble on until we could have a proper dinner later on.

Before long the room filled with the whirring noise of the printer as the scan information was transmitted to the roll of graph paper. Our eyes glowed and smiles appeared as different patterns became apparent on the paper strip. Something was there. Something was definitely there. We waited impatiently for all the scans to print out, which took the better part of an hour and two beers.

With the printing complete we stretched out the scrolled paper on the floor for study. The emerging pattern displayed many shades of gray. We were able to determine what we figured to be depth and varied densities of something under the desert sand. The four extreme ends being the lighter density with the center intersection area almost solid.

After toasting to our somewhat success Dan suggested we do some additional scanning tomorrow to fill in what we had not managed today. I wanted to just start digging but his logic made sense. We had a quick pizza supper and Dan left for home.

Alone now I stared at the paper mess on the floor, my imagination going wild.

"I'm sure the king could give me answers or at least hints." I muttered aloud to no one. "But it is no longer to be."

The tireds caught up with me and I threw myself on the bed without getting undressed. My mind ceased to function as I entered the land of nod.

~ ~ ~ ~ ~ ~

Once the scanning equipment was set up Dan and I went right to work filling in the missing areas of yesterday. An extra effort was concentrated on the two short sides of the intersection. Just after noon we finished our task and were enjoying cool refreshing water, satisfied with our efforts. As we viewed the horizon and beauty of the surrounds, Mr. Blue paid a visit again. His wandering journey ended about three feet from where we sat. He paused a few seconds then proceeded to dig into the sandy surface. After working to a depth of four inches or so he stopped and slowly retreated in the direction he came from.

Dan and I sat there dumbfounded staring at the creature till it was out of sight. Laughing at ourselves we began packing up our gear.

Satisfied there was nothing left behind we were about to enter the truck when I had this sudden urge to look at the small hole my Mr. Blue was digging.

For no apparent reason I reached down and with my hands started scooping more sand away. Approximately a foot deep my hand struck something small and hard. I excitedly dug around the object and pulled up what I thought was just a stone. I now had Dan's full attention. It wasn't a mere stone, it was a hunk of turquoise. A beautiful azure blue reflecting the midday sun. I brushed at it with the sleeve of my shirt. It was solid and pure with very little specs or flaws. I handed it to Dan who, polished it some more. He was all smiles as he commented;

"I thought you were off your rocker about that tarantula, but from now on I will pay a little more attention to them."

We both laughed as we continued to polish and view this new found treasure. Without a signal between us we dropped to our knees and extended outward and downward the spot Mr. Blue had shown us. There was nothing further to be found, like a couple of school boys we played catch with our blue stone on the way back to the truck.

"At least you now have a souvenir of your efforts." remarked Dan.

"But this is yours from your land." I argued.

"Don't be silly my friend, keep it. A memento of your trip. Something to tell your grand kids about. You know, your adventures with a blue tarantula." he chided.

Back at my rooms we set up immediately to post process our collected data. What we saw was beyond our expectations. The scan sheets filled in our missing data. We now had before us a definite picture. Of what we did not know, but it was a definite outline. We were looking at a square of approximately thirty meters a side encompassing a heavier density in the middle. Extending outward from the middle of each side was a leg of lesser density we guessed to be four meters by twelve meters before it faded out to register as sand. This was not a natural formation by our limited geological knowledge. But what was it ?

I hesitated before posing the next question to Dan.

"Can we dig ? At least a test dig ?" I qualified.

"I'm with you on that my friend." He said smiling, "But..."

With that my hopes dropped.

" I need some official approval first. I know it will not be a problem but even I have to play by the rules. We're probably looking at two days most."

I knew he was right, I was just over anxious. I believe Dan was as anxious as I. We forced ourselves to relax and discussed some preliminary plans.

Chapter 10

Dan returned to his other studies while I spent the same two days back at the desert indulging in my first love, photography. Convinced I had just taken the photo of a lifetime I would turn and see one better. This seemed to go on continuously. If only the world could see this never ending beauty. It's a wonder any one ever gets anything done in this part of the country.

My beauty parade finally ended with a call from Dan advising me that we got a green light for a test dig. He sounded more enthused about in than I did. He agreed to meet me there at eight the next morning and would bring whatever digging tools he thought necessary. The excitement made for a restless night but I did manage some sleep.

I arrived at our special site about twenty minutes early as did Dan. We laughed at each others anxiousness. As we were unpacking the digging tools my friend the Blue Tarantula showed up moving to the center of the intersection of choice. There he proceeded to dig. He went down about four inches then wandered away.

Smiling Dan said;

"**I** suppose that is where you plan on starting ?"

"**W**hy not." I answered, "He hasn't done me wrong yet."

Joking now we both walked to the chosen spot. The digging started relatively easy but the deeper we went the harder the earth. True it was mostly sand but it had been packed down for many centuries. By noon we had quite a hole which netted us absolutely nothing.

After a well earned lunch break we decided on probing with a piece of rebar Dan had on the truck. It was about twelve feet long. Our digging had already put us down approximately ten feet. Between the two of us muscling the rebar we managed to get it started into the ground. We then rigged up a platform to enable us to use a sledge hammer to pile drive. Our probe kept inching down which became rather frustrating and almost disheartening. With only about two feet left we struck something solid. We took turns pounding to no avail. We gained no more ground. Tired and sweaty we took a water break our hopes now renewed. We agreed to call it a day, deciding a backhoe was in order.

Again Dan reaffirmed there would be no problem. We gave ourselves a long rest before packing up our gear. We parted company with high hopes for tomorrow.

I treated myself to a dinner out then placed a call to Diego to thank him for the contact with Dan. There was no answer. I'll try again tomorrow although chances are they already left for the Yucatan.

For whatever reason I don't know but I slept late, skipped the call to Diego, and went straight to the desert.

Dan was already there with backhoe in tow. I made my apologies for being tardy and sported a huge smile at seeing the backhoe.

"I always wanted to operate one of these." I said.

"Who knows, today may be your chance." he returned.

As we each finished our coffee Dan turned slightly more serious.

"I did some thinking last night. Remembering those plots and the densities they showed, triggered some old thoughts. Some old oral legends tell of trade between our people and golden ones to the south. There were tales of large buildings with points. This got me thinking of pyramids, buildings with points. Now imagine if you will, viewing a pyramid from atop, density wise only. The heaviest concentration of the thickness or density is at the point. It then gradually lessons as you go out from the point."

My mind was going wild picturing the plots we had made. Dan's description fit like a glove. I did not dare though to dream of finding an actual pyramid even though by now I was familiar with them. But his theory was intriguing. Dan could see I was drifting and smiling said;

"I guess my wild thinking is contagious. You're caught up in it too. So where does that leave us ?"

"I know just where that leaves us now." I guess I piqued Dan's interest. You could tell he was waiting for more. "Yesterday we could only go so deep with the rebar. If we move away from center X amount of feet we should be able to go deeper, based on your theory."

"That makes sense so far." commented Dan.

I continued, "Let's try the rebar first before we start up the backhoe."

"Makes sense again. Based on the plots we may have an

 upside down funnel shaped structure. Let's try it"

Moving away from center ten feet we did the rebar routine again. We were successful this time. We were able to sink it about eight feet before hitting a solid barrier. Tired but happy we rested.

Smirking more than smiling Dan queried;

"Perhaps we should wait for your friend before we...." He stopped mid sentence staring past me. I turned my attention to that direction and sure enough there was my furry friend digging in the desert roughly twelve feet from center.

"I guess we start twelve feet away instead of ten feet." I said thank you to my blue friend as he casually wandered away.

"Seeing is believing but I go along with it anyway." said a smiling Dan.

Smiling also I said, "I'm not proud, I go with whatever works. Let's try the rebar where my blue friend indicated."

Lone buffalo joined me in the sinking of the bar. Much to the surprise of both of us the rebar sunk another four plus feet. The additional two feet from center made quite a difference. As an afterthought we both agreed upon checking the sonar plots again. Sure enough it appeared to validate what we just discovered with the rebar.

"Time to bring in the big guns." Dan suggested.

"Right you are my friend, I hope you know how to work that thing."

"Not to worry, I grew up with one of these. It helped pay my way through college."

The pair carefully unhooked the tie downs and soon the machine was in place. It was agreed only small bites would be taken until they could ascertain what, if anything, was underground.

Slow and methodically the claw did it's job. An eight foot swath was taking shape. Satisfied with the eight foot width they just kept digging it longer and longer to make it easier to walk.

An hour and a half and then some, of careful and frustrating digging they took a break. They rested at the farther edge of the digging area looking toward the center.

A light wind started, enough to disturb some of the newly loosened sand. Both Dan and I watched as the wind moved the sand at it's will. I imagined the shaping of the large sandstone sculptures standing guard in the desert was accomplished the same way eons ago. As the wind increased it's intensity, the sand obeyed and moved every which way till finally we were watching sand colored earth that was not moving. We looked at each other, questioning. Turning back to the excavated area, astonished, we watched more sand moving and slowly exposing a man made wall of earth colored stone and mud brick . The exposed area was growing bigger as it angled down away from the center. I was feeling the same chills I felt in the Yucatan every time we located a new structure or pyramid. Gazing back at Dan I saw his face wrinkled with smiles of wonderment. We dared not move from the scene being played out before us. The wind gusts moved on over the desert leaving an exposed wall section calling to us in the now quiet desert.

What we saw was about ten feet deep getting wider as it went down. Simultaneously we called to each other. "It's like a pyramid wall." We moved to the exposed wall, touching what had not been touched in who knows how long. Our first estimate was correct, this was a crude form of adobe brick. Crude or not they were fitted together perfectly. Now on our hands and knees we began scooping the dirt and sand away to expose more. It just appeared to go on and on. Dan went back to the truck for a couple of hand shovels. We continued for a while then decided to risk the backhoe again. We would just be more careful and dig more slowly.

At one point, for some unknown reason, I looked up toward the top of the hole. There, as if supervising, sat my furry blue friend. He stayed for almost ten minutes, then finally sauntered off. Dan just smiled shaking his head.

The initial shock of seeing the wall finally wore off and we both approached slowly. In unison our hands reached out to touch this mystery of the past. The sandpaper feel was magic to us. We were like giddy children touching everything we could.

Fun and games over we returned to the backhoe. This time we were even more careful. As we dug we kept moving back to allow for the slope of the pyramid. By mid afternoon there seemed to be no more wall. We were just moving dirt and sand. "Could this be the bottom ?"

Peering upward we guessed we were twenty feet deep. Backing out the machine we returned to the shovels. This time we moved parallel along the wall. We were looking for an opening. We actually reached a corner but still no opening.

Not wanting to stop we immediately started moving sand again. Time moved faster then we did and before we knew it dark had pushed the sun away.

Disappointed yet still exhilarated we quit for the day already looking forward to tomorrow.

The drive home alone seemed to last forever, my mind running wild. Not even thinking about what I was doing I mentally reached out to the king. Disheartened by not receiving an answer I scolded myself for being so stupid.

"Of course the king won't answer, he is long gone and it's time you let go."

Believe it or not I did feel better chastising myself. Smiling again and thinking about dinner I soon arrived home. A frozen Hungry Man Dinner and a cold beer and all was right with my world again, and it suddenly became a tired one. Between the mental excitement and physical activity, my body was sending me a message. Into bed I fell and out went my lights.

~ ~ ~ ~ ~ ~

I awoke at seven and realized it was still dark.
"That's funny, it should be well past sunrise." I thought.

I parted the curtains only to see dark clouds and heavy rain. I turned to the TV to catch the weather. Sure enough this was one of those rare desert storms, the length of which was unpredictable.

The blues hit my mood just as the telephone rang. Lone Buffalo was as depressed as I was. On a positive note he said the rain would give him a chance to catch up on other neglected projects. We would just have to wait out the storm.

Resigned to my fate I took my time fixing a full wholesome breakfast thinking about what to do with my idle time.

Checking at the motel office I inquired about a local library. About a forty minute drive there was such a place.

"Not very big, I'm afraid, we're just a small town." commented the motel manager.

What choice did I have, what else am I going to do in the rain.

~ ~ ~ ~ ~ ~

I was quite surprised at what I found. A quaint old adobe building larger than I expected. It had the usual set up with a surprising number of books and much to my delight a small section in the back dedicated to history of the Four Corners area.. This was right up my alley and before long I was up to my shoulders in books and maps of the area of my interest. I thought about my find, really Mr. Blues find, of the beautiful hunk of turquoise and decided to research that for a while.

I was amazed at the quantity of information available. This was all relatively new to me., ranging from light blue through blue, blue green, green and even brown. I was accustomed to seeing only blue. Once in a while something with dark streaks running through.

As I read on, the world of turquoise opened before me, showing me little facts unknown to most I assumed. Such as the green color because of the amount of iron content, while the blue was influenced by copper content in the stone.

Further reading explained that American turquoise is considered to be the finest in the world.

You learn something every day I thought. Apparently there was extensive trade with Mexico going way back in time.

I wondered if our friend, the king, was part of that. I do recall seeing quite an amount of turquoise stones among his possessions.

My chosen reading material was so fascinating time actually flew by. Before I knew it the librarian was notifying me that they were closing at five P.M.. I looked at my watch reading four forty five. It would take me fifteen minutes just to return all the books to their shelving.

I left this wonderful library, promising to return, with a handful of notes and copies of certain pages of interesting articles on turquoise.

These had nothing to do with my research of ancient roads in the desert yet I was more than pleased with myself with what I found. A note to myself to ask Lone Buffalo about turquoise.

Though it was still raining I felt accomplished from my time at the library. I even allowed myself a movie on TV before turning in for the night.

Reminiscent of the Yucatan, I awoke to more rain. I still felt good about yesterday but seeing the rain was depressing. *"Another trip to the library."* I thought as I fixed breakfast. While burning the bacon the phone rang. Dan's pleasant voice was loud and clear. He was more upbeat than I was even even with the rain. As if he could read my mind, he invited me to spend the day with him. Naturally I jumped at the chance, and by ten fifteen I was knocking at his office door.

His office was not what I expected. His desk, if it really was one, was a heap of papers, maps and photo's with a few rocks thrown in. The walls were nothing but push pins and pictures, both new and old. Smack dab in the middle of this organized clutter was an original Frederick Remington oil painting. It was the highlight of the office. Like a magnet it drew me across the room.

"That happens to everybody." smiled Dan. "That was a gift to my great, great grandfather from Remington himself and the painting is of my grandfather. It is something we are all very proud of."

"As well you should be." I agreed.

After ten minutes of the painting history, Lone Buffalo suggested I follow him through a typical day of his. I was quick to answer yes with a silly grin crossing my face.

The day was certainly worth while, to me anyway. Without going into too much detail, it covered his small teaching class, work in the artifact laboratory, document research, and answering mail requests for historical information. Because of the rain there were no site visits that were part of his history.

His teaching class fascinated me the most. His students were young teens, there to learn not only their cultural history but to learn how to further preserve it. These were the archeologists and anthropologists of the future.

By the time we left the class even I was more enthused about his disappearing history.

"It really must be preserved." I thought.

The day, being as busy as it was, flew by and before I was aware, it was after five in the afternoon. Dan and I went out for dinner at a local Taco place and I must admit I was surprised. It was nothing like the fast food places back east. This was the real thing.

It was still raining though it was lighter. The last forecast Dan heard for the next few days was clearing and clear with lots of sun. Based on this we made our plans for our return to Mr. Blue's special place. Dan had to finish up one project so we agreed not to meet till after nine in the morning.

We parted, both filled with anticipation. A cognac topped off my evening once I arrived back at my humble motel. I did some reading and fell asleep in the chair.

I surprised myself when I awoke still in the chair with the sun already leaking through the curtains. It was seven thirty which was rather late for me but there was still time for a shower and breakfast.

On the drive to the site I wondered what damage the rain would have done and how much re-digging we would have to do. I arrived about nine forty five and sat in the car a few minutes afraid to face the results of the rain. Scolding myself for being childish I finally got out of the car. Just as I closed the door Lone Buffalo showed up.

"I can't wait to see how we fared in the storm." he commented as he headed straight for the dig. I hurried to catch up with him hiding my embarrassment. We both stopped at the same time, mouth's open, gawking at our angled wall. The rain had fully exposed the corner where we quit the other day. Not only the corner but a good part of the second wall. This was truly a pyramid from what we could see. A low one but a pyramid nonetheless.

As we moved to the newly exposed wall the sand gave way under our feet causing a mini slide. Not only down but across the newly exposed wall. We tried to move closer to no avail. Try walking up at a steep angled sand pile, there is no footing. We resigned ourselves that it was back hoe time again.

In twenty minutes we were in position and ready for our first scoop. Dan picked a spot and with precise movement carefully attacked the sand at the base of the second wall. Moving ever so slowly he backed the jaws down and away causing a mine slide again, in turn exposing more wall. I nodded the okay for a second scoop and Dan carried out my wish with the same results, a continual slide of sand. Only this time the displacement was greater. So mich so that an opening made itself known. Again we gaped in awe, our hearts beating like drums. We dared another swipe with the hoe netting the desired effect.

Now there before us was a rectangular opening about four feet wide and probably six feet high. We stood there frozen like two kids at a magic show. Who knows how long we would have stayed like that but for my furry blue pal. He appeared at the top of the wall moving to the opening mantle and proceeded to crawl inside.

"I wish I could walk upside down like that. The king would probably say I could." I thought to myself.

Dan and I looked at each other, smiled, then proceeded to crawl up the sand slope to the entrance. It was a bit of a struggle but we finally made it. We now stood at the entrance looking at nothing but dark. We laughed at our own foolishness for not thinking about a lantern or flashlight. Dan volunteered to go back to the truck returning with both items. In the meantime I dared to enter the unknown. Feeling my way along, the walls were amazingly smooth. I was about eight feet in and completely surrounded by darkness. I reversed my course and headed for what little light I could see. I exited at the same time Dan returned.

"What did you find out." asked Dan anxiously.

"Not a damn thing." I answered smiling. "It's darker then night in there."

Dan grinned as he handed me the lantern keeping the flashlight for himself.

Now properly prepared we nodded to each other and entered the past. The walls and ceiling were smooth as I had discovered earlier only now that we were deeper the ceiling was noticeably lower. It reduced to about five feet for reasons unknown, but I'm sure there must have been a purpose. Reaching what appeared to be the center of the pyramid the area opened up again. We were now in an open chamber roughly fifteen by fifteen feet, each side having a passage way similar to the one we just navigated.

Dead center is what piqued our interest. A support structure, four feet square holding rope cables on a pulley system to hoist a platform up and down.

Simultaneously we both mumbled aloud; "Mine shaft."

Cautiously moving closer for a better look we inched our way to the edge. Peering down into darkness again. Dan moved his flashlight to a better position but all we could see was cable supports.

We backed off both remaining silent. Not really knowing what to do I held up the big lantern moving it around to show more of the other three passage ways.

"Why not." said Dan and moved toward the one on his right. I followed close behind holding the light up high to illuminate our way. Except for the dust of age the hallway was clean. The dimensions pretty much like our entranceway. Then it just ended. No door or hatch, just solid wall. I remembered Carlos and his looking for opening wedges or hooks or sliding stones. I proceeded to try the same much to the confusion of Lone Buffalo.

"I'll explain later." I said as I kept feeling and looking.

I quit after ten minutes feeling frustrated.

"What was that all about." smiled Dan.

I then quickly related my Carlos story of how we entered the Mayan ruins.

"Oh." Dan said straight faced not knowing whether to believe me or not.

I left it at that and walked to the next tunnel, which was a repeat of the one we just left. Nothing. The third and last were the same. Why a passageway to nowhere ? We had no clue.

Back to the vertical shaft, both thinking the same. It had to be investigated but could the rope be trusted to hold and not send us to our death. We dared not trust it. Suddenly Dan remembered he had both new rope and steel cable in the truck.

"We could rewire the shaft box to our satisfaction." He said excitedly.

A little over an hour later we were set. Even the extra length of cable was secured to the backhoe for added safety. It was then decided only one should descend the shaft with the other staying up on level ground again for safety sake. Lone Buffalo insisted it be me who goes down first since this whole thing was my project. I wasn't about to argue

I entered the crudely made box and with a secondary rope around my waist we started my descent, my lantern continually searching the shaft walls and the unknown hollow below. Dan was slowly lowering the box listening to my commands.

"Stop." I yelled.

I brought the lantern closer to the shaft wall. *"Could it be ?"* I asked myself.

"What's up ?" Dan shot down.

"It looks like gold. Is that possible ?" I answered.

"Why not, there used to be a lot of gold mining in these parts." Dan replied. "It never amounted to super riches though."

"This is a zig zag strip about four inches wide in the wall, as if they just left it there." I explained back.

"I'm sure they did." Dan said. "They were most likely after something more valuable."

"What's more valuable than gold." I shouted back.

"I'm sure you will find out, just keep going." ha answered matter of factly. As he continued the lowering process.

"I'll explain later." I heard him add.

Down we went into the darkness , the smell of ancient, damp earth permeated my nostrils. It was rather obvious this shaft had not been open for who knows how many years, perhaps even centuries.

The ropes suddenly slackened. I had hit bottom. I scanned three hundred sixty degrees with my lantern. I was in an open space about ten feet square. There were horizontal running shafts in the center of each wall approximately the same position as the tunnels up at the entrance topside. I tried shouting up to Dan with no success, I was just too deep. Letting my curiosity take over, I climbed out of the basket and walked to one of the tunnels. The lantern showed nothing but more black.

I dared to enter and after about ten or twelve feet I was able to make out ruts in the hardened dirt floor, parallel ruts. The kind you would use for a cart of sorts. *"A mining cart, of course"* I scolded myself.

Continuing forward I could tell the tunnel now had a downward bent. I also picked up a sparkle on the floor every now and then. I stopped for a closer look. Turquoise !   I held in my hand a hunk of turquoise the size of a baseball. I went forward another twenty or so steps and found myself in an open area of no particular dimension with walls of jagged rock. Not so much rock as it was turquoise. Pure turquoise. I was surrounded by it. I wanted to shout with happiness. In fact I did, then turned around to make sure no one was looking. I don't think anyone has seen this much turquoise in their whole lifetime except of course these original miners.

This wasn't a pyramid for religious observances, but a building hiding and housing a mine and it's entrances and shafts. I dallied a while then remembered poor Dan above ground, waiting anxiously.

I returned to the vertical shaft, climbed into the box and proceeded to hoist myself up. Dan joined in from topside which made the job easier.

Like an excited school child I related my story as soon as I caught sight of him. He was all smiles and giggles as he tried to slow me down.

"I had my suspicions this is what you would find." he said as I struggled with the chunk in my pocket.

I mentioned I had only looked in one tunnel but thought he might want the honor of doing the others. We finally decided the rope and pulley system we hooked up would hold us both, so down we went.

~ ~ ~ ~ ~ ~

-The Ancient Ones-

The tunnel one hundred and eighty degrees opposite the one I searched was blocked with rock, dirt and chunks of turquoise. We decided it was a cave in. We moved on to the other two and found the same thing I viewed in the first. I don't know too much about turquoise mines but from what I saw, this was a large find.

Time was fleeting, it was already late afternoon and we called it quits for the day.

Dan posted signs, you know, keep out, private, Native American property etc. We then tarped the entrance as best we could as a further deterrent. We rested a while making plans for tomorrow and for obtaining access to the fourth tunnel..

We each went our own way and I was glad to be home, motel though it was. I was still excited and quite tired, although it was a good tired.

In awe of my hunk of blue rock, I fondled and gazed at it all through my Hungry Man dinner. Regretfully I put it aside and hit the pillow.

~ ~ ~

The sun had me up early looking forward to today's digging. I assumed this fourth tunnel would be a copy of the other three, but I let my imagination run away with my mind. They always get along well with each other. I pictured hidden rooms as in the kings tomb and perhaps some of his texts. I really do know how to get carried away. I cleaned up after breakfast and aimed the car for the "Home of my furry blue friend."

Dan was already there, calmly waiting for me. This time he managed to bring along a generator and plenty of electric cable to have a better system of lighting.

Once down and in front of the cave in we started moving rock, sand and dirt. Moving the boulders was hard enough but the bigger problem was where to put the debris. We were running out of room in our shallow space. Taking a break we threw ideas at each other. The only one that made sense would be the most difficult one, yet it was the only way to gain the space needed.

Finally agreeing we started the long and tedious job of loading rocks in the shaft cart and lifting them up to ground level. This meant, of course, one of us would have to remain below and one topside to empty the cart.

The system was working but we knew it would take twice

the time. Resigning ourselves to that fact did, however, help the time pass. We switched positions every now and then to even out the work load. Not realizing we forgot about lunch completely, then suddenly it was dark.

We assessed our progress, or lack thereof only to find we had opened about eight feet. It was a thorough eight feet though we weren't just making a crawl space.

Settled comfortably on the desert again, Lone Buffalo voiced the obvious.

"We need help."

Laughing, I looked at him saying,

"Do you really think so ?"

He got my message and laughed along with me. Out of the clear blue I heard,

"My class ! They are way overdue for some field work."

"I'll even provide them with lunch if you think that would help."

"Lunch and pizza when we finish." Dan threw in.

"I'll throw that in too." I smiled.

By the time I finished talking Dan was already on his cell phone making the arrangements. I would take care of the food, both lunch and pizza on the way back to the motel. There was a decent sized diner just a few miles from my lodgings. I also remembered a pizza house I passed on my way to the library.

With renewed energy we closed up our pyramid mine and parted company, anticipating a good day tomorrow.

As I was walking back to my car my blue tarantula crossed my path, stopped as if looking at me with approval then meandered on his way. I smiled, feeling good inside, and started for home.

Chapter 11

The phone ringing awakened me. My watch showed seven thirty two which the sun streaming in through the curtains confirmed. It was Lone Buffalo with an update on our chosen volunteer labor force. They probably would not be there until ten thirty-ish. That was fine with me I told him. That gave me the time I needed to arrange for lunch and pizza supper.

I managed to make my food arrangements and still arrive at our special site just after ten. As scheduled Dan showed at ten thirty followed by a small bus. There were eight teens and two older chaperones. Dan explained he only wanted the older teens for safety sake because of the inherent danger of the mine. The chaperones for obvious reasons.

We went right to work with four young men top side with an adult and four below with an adult. Dan and I took turns for both up and down to supervise the removal and re-stacking of the cave in debris. The teens worked well and non-stop. Their enthusiasm and concern showed. After all it was their past they were working for.

A mini van with lunch makings appeared on the dot of one P.M.. Lunch was devoured with the same enthusiasm the kid's showed in their work and were more than willing to get back to the job at hand.

By three thirty a record amount of rock and earth had been removed to a point where Dan and I called it quits. I explained to him of my experience in the Yucatan of the stale air problems upon the opening of the tomb. He agreed not to expose the young ones to that risk. We would allow them to come back at another time to view the fruits of their labor.

The clean up for the day also went well much to the disappointment of the younger set. They were anxious to see what was behind the cave in. It sure was great to have that extra help.

The pizza for dinner party was a great success. I didn't care about the bill. I felt it was worth every penny. With only Dan and I clearing the debris it would have taken many days.

Anxious for tomorrow I went to bed immediately on my

return from dinner.

~ ~ ~

It was barely sunup as I was making my self a breakfast sandwich. My coffee thermos was already filled along with the water jug. I watched the sky change colors as I drove to the desert proper. I still got the chills through out watching the changing beauty of the sandstone sculptures as the sun and shadows played tag on the rough edges. My so-called breakfast finished I poured a second cup of coffee and slowly walked the edges of the rock pile built by the kids. Here and there small pieces of turquoise showed from their stone hosts. A touch of gold could also be detected now and then.

I was trying to picture in my mind the cave in of the tunnel way back then. We were cleaning the rubble away. Why didn't they ? Everything else was neat and clean yet the cave in was left as is. Note to self, ask Dan if he has the means to date the mine and it's covering structure. I continued sipping my coffee staring at the disorganized rock pile when low and behold my furry blue companion approached on the top stone. No longer ashamed of myself for talking aloud to creatures and inanimate objects I addressed Mr. Blue.

"Good morning Mr. Blue, how is the world treating you. I'll bet you know the king. You must, since you have been giving me all the this help. Next time you see him give him my regards."

I smiled getting the sense he was watching and listening to me. We were both frozen in place staring as if probing each others mind. Something told me to break this stand off. As I did my furry friend crawled down the debris pile and without hesitation entered the pyramid. I watched until he disappeared in the darkness. I shook myself back to a sense of reality as Lone Buffalo arrived.

We filled the generator with gas and fired it up lighting the shaft and tunnel. Once below ground we went right to work. Within an hour we felt we were at the point of breaking through. Because of my previous experience I had us both tie dampened bandanas around our noses and mouth.

Working together we pried a good sized boulder free from the grip of the others. We jumped aside as it fell turning away from the opening as stale air rushed out. We moved back to the shaft area and waited about ten minutes.

We slowly retraced our path to the tunnel opening. We

peeked in using only the lantern but failed to see anything of significance. Disappointment showing on our faces we set about clearing a larger opening for easier entrance and egress, then reorganized our electric cable for maximum illumination in the newly opened tunnel.

The air had cleared enough to remove our masks. In we went dragging along our lighting. We found ourselves in a large well mined area at least forty feet square, most of which were stacked with piles of almost pure turquoise. There was even one row dedicated to just gold with some copper mixed in.

Dan and I gaped at our surrounds in wonderment. With all this at their disposal why was no attempt made to clear away the cave in ? A big question with no apparent answer. Dan spoke a little of the oral history of this blue stone called turquoise. It was all said matter of factly. I made him agree to fill me in with more detail at another time.

We eventually found the will to move and each aimed for a different row. Almost simultaneously each called out to the other. I found a poor soul who did not make it out of the room. I was looking at a skeleton of a Native American, dried shrunken skin fully clothed in what I considered clothing of the time. But what time ?

Dan defined the exact same thing to me except he was using the word Zuni and Anasazi for the dead ancestor. Again we agreed to discuss those details later. Neither looked as if they had struggled and they were many, many feet from the mine opening.

We continued our investigation of the other aisles amazed at the quantity of turquoise. Even more amazed at the apparent quality. The next to last isle showed us another workers skeleton. This one was facing away from the tunnel, a huge piece of gold remained in his hand. Dan than determined he was carrying it to a rear stack which appeared to be all gold.

In the far corner of the room at the end of the last row we found two more full skeletons in the same state of preservation, yet something was different. Dan and I each observed these two slowly trying to determine what difference we could detect. The familiarity suddenly dawned on me. These two were not Native American. At least not of North America.

Their attire was Mayan. Upon closer examination they were Maya from the Yucatan. How could I be so sure ? I just spent two summers with their king. Their dress bore a significant resemblance to that of the king, including the red feathers. I pointed out the things I was familiar with to Dan who was more than interested.

We each heard of trading between Mexico and the Four

Corners area but this was an additional surprise.

We conducted additional searches of the complete room to find nothing else outstanding.

The dating question was now the utmost importance to both of us. This small find could again alter some of our early history as we now know it.

We could sense the lights flickering which meant we were running low on fuel. We were forced to quit for the day.

We offered a last prayer, so to speak, to our departed brethren and tarped over the tunnel entrance, then ascended to the desert level. Again we covered the pyramid entrance and closed the equipment boxes. We sat silently on the tailgate looking at the surrounding uniqueness, our thoughts moving to the ones forever locked inside the pyramid.

~ ~ ~ ~ ~ ~

Finding the mother lode of turquoise no longer was of major excitement. Our priority for the next few days was the proper reburial of our deceased mine workers according to custom. This was not just a case of a hole in the ground. Both lone Buffalo and I wanted to respect the customs of the time period, first we had to establish what it was, naturally for the Native Americans but for the Maya of the same period.

My acquaintances from my Yucatan experience would be invaluable. I would check with Mario and Diego first thing in the morning. Dan planned to go to the tribal elders for input.

Though our intention was to release news of our find, we considered it premature at this time. We did not need a flood of people interfering with what we considered our humble and necessary duty. We each left for our respective residences with my promise to go to Dan's office as soon as I gathered the information I needed from my Maya colleagues

My night was somber not being able to erase the thoughts of those five dedicated men. There appeared to be no effort to clear away the rubble of the collapse from either side. This was the most curious of events that bothered me. "WHY?" I resigned myself to the fact that it was something we would never know.

Chapter 12

"No, we didn't leave yet, it looks like it may be a few more weeks. We have some more coordinating to do with the authorities of Mexico. No real problem, just a delay." explained Mario. "You're up pretty early, what can I do for you."

"It's good to hear your voice again." I replied. "I have a rather delicate situation here and I would like your input."

"Of course, Eric, anything you need if I'm able."

I explained my last few days to Mario emphasizing the Mayan presence. His voice more serious now, Mario proposed;

"I'm glad for the delay now. Let me know exactly where you are and Diego and I will be there tomorrow. Your sensitivity is of great comfort to me." In a lighter tone he added, "I always knew you had some Maya blood."

I felt honored with his remark. We completed our details and said our so longs for the time being. I finished my coffee and drove to Lone Buffalo's office.

Dan tied up some loose ends of his teaching class while waiting for me. In a bit of a hurry, we jumped into his truck, taking about a fifteen minute drive to the meeting with the elders. I let my imagination play tricks with my mind during the drive. I pictured a very large teepee with a central fire pit with many elderly men adorned in deer skin and buffalo robes, smoking long pipes. Each elder had a time to speak until a final consensus was reached.

When we reached our destination, I was brought back to reality. Here was a fairly modern school building which housed a formal meeting room. This special room held a long table fitted with twelve or so chairs, nine of which were already occupied. These elders, as it were, consisted of seven men and two women, dressed in modern attire accented by beautiful turquoise jewelry. What also surprised me was these elders, in my opinion were not really elderly. I judged early fifties to early sixties. My introduction was made and we explained my research which led to this mine and the ancestral skeletons.

Lone Buffalo petitioned for the proper service necessary for an honorable burial for the three ancestors. I then filled in with my information of the two deceased Mayans and my Mayan friends who were on their way.

The elders appeared pleased with my arrangements and briefly engaged in the discussions of ceremonial protocol. I was impressed with the dignity and compassion they showed. Pride in their heritage and for that of the Maya took center stage. It was a good feeling that there was still people who cared for and respected others.

Our mission with the elders completed we returned to Dan's office. We knew that work at the mine would be suspended for a few days. Burial ceremonies naturally took priority.

Dan discussed some background of turquoise with me. He spoke of the Cerrillos mine in New Mexico. It was considered the oldest mine of any mine in North America. Eventually it had the reputation of also being the site of the largest prehistoric mining activity on the continent with obvious trade with the peoples of Mexico. This particular mine provided not only turquoise, but gold, silver and copper. It was the largest, until now perhaps, joked Dan.

I filled Dan in on another mine he was not aware of. A copper mine by Lake Michigan and Superior. It had been dated back to twenty four hundred BC. The mine was worked for over sixteen hundred continuous years. Millions of tons of copper were taken and shipped back to Europe and the Mediterranean area..

"Getting back to the present mine." Dan said "This mine of yours could be history changing. But first we have to finish our dating and historical research, not only of the mine but the structure housing it. Pyramid structures were not exactly known in North America."

"Perhaps when Diego and Mario arrive they can help with the dating of both." I posed.

"You're right." Dan exclaimed excitedly. "I forgot about the Maya connection. I know they have oral history as do we and between both I'm sure we can narrow down a date, at least to a century."

"I think we can probably even do better."

We were both excited now.

"There is nothing more we can do here until our Mayan friends get here. But what we can do to kill time and be constructive is return to the mine and get some samples of wood for dendrochronology.*

"Good thinking my friend." I congratulated Dan. "Now I feel like we're accomplishing something. Now is also when I wish the king was here. His wisdom was invaluable."

Dan smiled knowing my feelings and accepted me for them. He would fit in very well with the Maya. His compassion and enthusiasm for his heritage and the study and preservation of it was a most honorable treat.

Our leisurely drive to our mine location was pleasant, we were not under our own forced time restraints. We stood for a while before entering the pyramid, both thinking of the five that were buried alive. Without a word , just a nod of our heads we hesitantly entered. Firing up the generator gave us the light we needed. Surveying our immediate surrounds yielded nothing of significance. I looked to the elevator shaft but did not want to disturb that framing, we still required it's use. A slight movement caught my eye. Dan saw it also. My furry blue friend was moving up and down the wall of the shaft, only moving six or eight inches at a time as if trying to get our attention. Once he was sure he had it, which he did, he continued down the shaft. A silly grin appeared on both our faces.

"Why not." I said, "He hasn't steered me wrong yet."

Down our mine shaft elevator we went. Sure enough my blue friend was waiting. He crawled toward the first tunnel I had checked out. We overtook him going in and did not see him again for the rest of the day.

At the rear of this tunnel to nowhere were some old logs stacked against the side wall. A few were twelve or fourteen feet long mixed with a few pieces three to four feet in length. They appeared to be rather old and felt extremely dry. We carried a few pieces to better light and chose what we thought to be three different types of tree.

That whole process was short lived which meant we still had a good part of the day before us. We were both anxious to return to the mine itself but out of respect for the dead decided against it. After all these years the mine was not going any place.

We regretfully returned to Dan's office where he shared with me some historical documents of the Navaho and Anasizi. I found the material fascinating and tucked it away in my memory bank for future study. Perhaps another Eric Dexter adventure sortie, but that's for another time.

* Dendrochronology   is an absolute dating method based upon the patterns of tree ring growth.

-The Ancient Ones-

      I was surprised to read that the Navajo* (Navaho) was not in their language but came from the early Spaniards. They originally referred to themselves as "DINEH" (the people).

      The Anasizi material was sparse but interested me more, I guess because of the time period not firmly established. The word or name Anasizi has a few different meanings. Some refer to Ancient ones, others refer to Ancient Enemy. They settled the area of the four corners early, then seemed to have vanished. The popular consensus is that drought forced them to go further south or just move to better climes.. Their dwellings are a testament to their engineering skills evidenced by the historical archeological remains. Maybe, again wishful thinking, they were the early turquoise miners and their trade with peoples to their South was the cause of the Mayan presence. We may have some answers tomorrow from Mario and Diego. I sure am keeping my fingers crossed.

      The day seemed to drag. The reading material Dan shared with me helped pass the time, but the anticipation of tomorrow was almost too much to bear. By mid-afternoon I took my leave of Lone Buffalo and drove back to the desert. Not for more work or research, but to cleanse my mind. The jungle had its music while the desert has its color and light show. Right now I needed natures beauty to remind me how insignificant we humans are. The view of the sunset was like cleansing my soul.

      Feeling somewhat refreshed and at peace with myself I drove to my humble abode, but not before stopping for some Italian food to go. My pasta meal and a couple of glasses of wine completed my evening perfectly. I hit the pillow and don't remember a thing till my alarm welcomed me to the next day.

      I knew my Mayan friends were not due until noon-ish, so I poked around my motel suite reviewing my maps and measurements and plots. Everything checked out as far as I could tell, yet there was something that kept nagging at me. I could not put my finger on it, but there appeared to be something missing. I had no idea what. I could not take my eyes off my plot map. I knew I was in a trance like state but I couldn't move. My imagination superimposed a plot of the lost city in the Yucatan over my roadway map. Suddenly, there before me was something I should have picked up on earlier. The alignment of the pyramid housing the mine was in perfect harmony with the major tomb pyramid of the kings lost city.

      Why hadn't I recognized this before, I scolded myself. There was the Maya influence. If not the Maya, per se', it was an earlier culture that

---

* Navajo - loosely translated to mean large cultivated fields. (Farmers)

believed in the stars and moon and sun that gave life to everything here on earth.

No matter what period or culture you study, the stars placement in the heavens gave meaning and purpose to their lives. Without going into long winded detail the alignment of the early peoples temples, pyramids and tombs with the sun and or stars became a necessity in their life and beliefs.

With renewed enthusiasm I set out for Dan's office to await Mario and Diego's arrival. Dan was as excited as I was when I relayed the news of my discovery. He had read about and studied alignments yet had never actually come across anything in the studies of his own peoples. Yes the cardinal points were important but alignments were relatively new to him.

Lone Buffalo had brought some sandwiches and milk from home and since it was almost one P.M. we cleared a spot at the map table to partake in lunch. It was the perfect timing for our awaited guests to arrive. It was truly great to see then both again and double pleasure for Diego to be reunited with his old friend and classmate, Dan.

Once we finished with the hugs and backslaps the four of us enjoyed lunch, meager though it was, now being shared by four. Conversation was lively and interesting with the sharing of information of the upcoming Yucatan expedition and the details of our find of the unfortunate miners.

The mood took on a somber note as we all piled into Dan's truck and took off for the desert. Arrival at our place of interest needed no description. The sight of our mini pyramid captivated our mutual friends.

It was as if I could read their thoughts. Suddenly it dawned on me that I was reading their thoughts. The king had opened our minds to this method of communication. We expected it with the king but now our mutual surprise was evident. The three of us actually quietly smiled at each other with Dan none the wiser. We purposely kept our secret from Dan, for now anyway. No need to surprise him with too much right away.

Mario recalled hearing about such a small structure, once secreting and housing treasures and artefacts from the Spaniards. It also was buried underground.

We un-tarped the entrance and descended by twos to the lower shaft. Our guests marveled at the engineering feat considering the age. All four of us approached the tunnel of the cave in. Dan removed the tarp and brought in the lighting set up. As with Dan and I, the sight of all the turquoise and gold took their breath away although we remained silent. I led the way to our fallen Mayan comrades. I stepped aside with Dan and allowed Mario and Diego time with their ancestors. Mario finally broke the silence.

"I'm not exactly sure, but by their dress, I would say they were from a pre- classic period."

Diego concurred while already with his sketch pad and pencil.

"I can check for an exact date once I have access to some historic records."

"In the meantime what can we do for you now."

"I want to give Diego his time and then we would like to offer some prayers." I answered.

Dan joined in; "We are going to hold a parting ceremony for our three relatives. If you would allow us the honor we could hold a joint service."

"That would be most acceptable." replied Mario. "And more than appropriate I would think. They lived together, worked together and died together and thus it follows suit that they be interred together."

This pleased Dan as evidenced by his smile.

Diego terminated his sketching and joined us, also approving the plan of a joint ceremony.

Just before leaving I took some pictures for documentation purposes, with permission, of course.

Once back topside on the desert we outlined our plan. It was agreed that final plans would be made by the council of elders which was our next stop. Arrangements were also made for overnight quarters for Mario and Diego. They would be staying at reservation facilities courtesy of "The People"

The four of us had a catch up dinner then parted for the night. Relaxed and at peace with myself I slept like a baby that night.

~ ~ ~ ~ ~ ~

The parting ceremony was both solemn and joyous that the five miners were free and would be joining the Great Spirit of both of their worlds hereafter.

Mario tried to talk me into another Yucatan journey but I explained that I must finish this project first. He clearly understood. Dan made a presentation of about ten pounds of raw turquoise, with the blessing of the elders.

"Use this to help fund you research." He suggested. "We

obviously now have a permanent tie between our peoples. I just might like to join you myself on one of your expeditions."

"You will be more than welcome, my friend." answered Mario. "I think we would like that also. Perhaps you can convince this runaway to join you." he said smiling as he put his hand on my shoulder.

We all said our parting farewells and Dan and I watched them drive away with a trailing dust cloud."

Chapter   13

The burial of our ancient Colleagues took the better part of the day so Dan and I agreed not to return to the desert for such a short afternoon. Dan returned to his school while I drove to my comfy motel. I caught up on some reading and dozed off for the rest of the night.

The following day found me well rested yet with a touch of melancholy for the ancient ones we finally put to rest. For whatever reason as anxious as I was to get back to the desert mine, I just wasn't moving very fast. This fact bothered me that it didn't bother me. It all seemed anti-climatic at this point. I had discovered something new, it was valuable, it was historic and yet I felt unfulfilled; let down. Why should I feel let down ? Anybody else would be elated with what I accomplished and here I was feeling empty.

I packed up a few things and headed for the mine. I decided in my downed mood that if I wanted something new and different I would have to find it. I questioned myself though, *"What more historically could I expect after finding a Mayan - Native American connection.*

"Perhaps there is more to the connection than you realize, Eric."

The voice was familiar, but I was alone in the car.

It has been a long time my friend, it is good to hear your thoughts again. I see you have not been idle. It is good to see you still care about the past."

I could not believe my own thoughts. Pulling the car over for

-The Ancient ones-

safety sake I killed the engine to concentrate on the kings words.

"**I**s that really you ATAL or am I letting my mind play tricks in my head."

"Your mind, as your heart, Eric, is true. Diego relayed to me how you cared for my people. Only a true son of the world would have loved that much. Again it shows my reason for choosing you to be caretaker of the people."

"**I** remain flattered, ATAL, that you even considered me, but I still hold that burden is much too great for me."

"As you wish Eric." The king stated disappointedly.

"**T**ruth be told." I continued, "I didn't think I would ever talk with you again."

"Once Mario and Diego spoke of your mission I just knew I could be of assistance."

"**N**o disrespect meant Sir, but what knowledge do you have of these loving people."

"Ah, still the ever curious Eric." answered the king. *Perhaps you have forgotten, we have knowledge of all peoples."*

Embarrassed by my forgetfulness I inquired of the assistance the king offered. After all I had already uncovered a buried mine without his help, I think.

"I will go back to what I said previously Eric. Perhaps there is more to this connection than you realize. As you have learned from the past, Eric, the things you seek are always deeper than imagined."

The word imagined faded as he finished speaking. I knew from experience my moment with the king had ended for now."

I sat there for a few minutes, puzzled as usual by his riddles. With no instant answer I started the car and continued on to the mine.

I arrived at the pyramid sight to find Dan waiting.

"I figured you overslept." he said with a smile.

At first I didn't say anything. Why burden him with confusion. I then had second thoughts. I already told him of the king, why not keep him up to date ? I explained my tardiness relaying the king's riddle. Dan gave me a strange look, not sure what to believe any more. Casting off his doubts, he turned the conversation to the riddle.

"That should be simple enough. I would say we just have to dig deeper."

I looked at him, my expression blank.

"Deeper okay, but where and for what ?"

"Got me, Pal." answered Lone Buffalo. "Maybe your pet spider will show us." he remarked sarcastically.

I wanted to laugh but realized perhaps he was right..

*"**W**hat's come over me lately."* I thought. *"First I have the king directing me, now I'm allowing a tarantula to lead me. Get a hold of yourself Eric. So far both of the above have been true to you."*

I smiled at Dan with a suggestion we go down into the mine.

As we climbed onto the platform and took hold of the ropes to descend we were followed by Mr. Blue.

Now I was being really freaked out. Did I have any private thoughts of my own any more.

When we touched down Dan and I stepped aside to allow Mr. Blue to exit first. Smiling, almost laughing, we followed to the turquoise treasure room. Dan saw to the lighting hook up and as the lights brightened we watched my furry blue friend disappear under the middle pile of turquoise. Lone Buffalo looked at me questioningly as I shrugged my shoulders. We waited a few minutes but he did not return. Our curiosity piqued, we wandered to the aisle in question with Dan now on hands and knees.

"Will you look at that ?" he softly said. "There's a wooden structure under this pile of stone. Almost like a platform."

Now I also lowered to my hands and knees small flashlight in tow. With more light on the subject we could see it was more than a simple structure.

We sat back looking at this six foot by ten foot by six foot high pile of raw turquoise. If we wanted to satisfy our curiosity we would have to move it. Talk about putting a damper on your spirits, this pile of blue rock did just that.

"It's still early." said Dan smiling.

We both knew we would do it no matter the time.

Dan rearranged the lighting and we started. Piece by piece. I then realized the logistics of where to put the stone was a problem. As I gazed around for the solution I heard Dan.

"No need for that my friend."

Turning I saw Dan holding a section of board to which were attached large and small stones of blue and blue green. On closer inspection the whole pile was false. This was a housing cloaking a cover to something below.

As the beam from the flashlight uncovered the details we saw Mr. Blue scurry away, apparently his job finished for this day anyhow.

We removed more of this outer housing, both being puzzled by the method of adhering the stone to the wood. At our quick glance clarity was not forthcoming.

Our attention was now really focused on the door in the floor. This was not wood but stone of some sort. It was something much harder than the surrounding desert sand stone.

Once the dust of the ages was swept away we stood mesmerized by what was before us. We were looking at Glyphs. I don't know how long we stared till it finally dawned on me to exercise my profession.

I retrieved my camera, adjusted the lights and clicked away from all angles. I just wished I could read the Glyphs.

Dan waited patiently while I played photographer all the while trying to figure a way to open this floor door. The camera put away I joined Dan at the stone door, both of us now using the fingertip method as employed by Carlos in the Yucatan.

Ten minutes passed with no results from either of us. I sat back frustrated. Suddenly I recalled the kings words, *"The things you seek are always deeper than imagined."*

My eyes went instantly to the Glyphs. There were three in a vertical row running length wise in the five foot or so door. The middle was extremely intricate with a deep recess in the center. Sporting a half smile I extended my finger and explored the recess. Feeling resistance I heard a click. More like a heavy thud.

Dan was smiling from ear to ear.

Together we tried to lift the door. It did not budge. Remembering the kings pyre I indicated to Dan we try to slide it. Both pushing from one end again netted us zero. Dan suggested an angle push. Bingo! It moved quite effortlessly to reveal a rough cut stone stairway rather steep looking. Holding the lantern over the opening showed a non ending mass of curved steps and darkness.

Dan and I stepped back to assess what now faced us. As earlier we chose to let air equalize itself with fresh air. We were silent, thinking, questioning, and imagining. Dan stirred first quietly asking;

"Who first ?"

"It's your land. " I answered.

"Yes, but it's your dream." he smiled.

Without answering I stood and approached the steps, lantern in hand. I watched the eery shadows run before me as the lantern swayed in my hand. The rock steps became steeper, the curved wall tightened it's circle. I took each step slower and more carefully as the rocks became less even and much more jagged. I laughed quietly to myself as I heard Dan cuss softly having stepped the wrong way on a ragged edge.

The air was still a bit stagnant and heavy so I stopped my descent. Dan caught up to me but neither of us chose to speak because of the air quality. We both tied our bandana's around nose and mouth. It seemed to help.

The light desert breeze acted as a suction draft, drawing the stale air up and out. Within five or six minutes we resumed our downward trek.

The rise of each step was far from constant but I judged us to be about twenty plus feet down as we leveled off. An extremely narrow corridor faced us, not made for people over five foot ten.

We slowly negotiated the passageway which angled slightly to our right after ten or so feet. Another fifteen feet brought us to a stone portal beyond which a heavy wooden door could be seen.

I took a step toward the wood barrier then suddenly stopped. Dan almost bumped into ne because I stopped so suddenly.

"What's wrong ?" he asked

-The Ancient Ones-

"I don't know," I answered. "Something funny about the portal."

We both backed up a few steps. I gazed up to what caught my my eye just seconds ago. My eyes did not deceive me. I was looking at Glyphs. Mayan Glyphs. Dan aimed his flashlight more directly at the lintel.

"Is that what I think it is?" he quizzed.

"Yes, it is my friend. Another piece of history has just been revealed to us." I said excitedly.

His smile went from ear to ear.

"Can you read them." he asked hurriedly.

"I wish I could." I answered sadly.

I had Dan direct the light to a certain spot.

"That part I recognize as a number but which one I don't know."

"Perhaps it's time for Mario and Diego to return." suggested Lone Buffalo

"Not a bad idea but I'm sure by now they're on their way to the lost city."

"Are you sure of that my young friend ?"

I turned to see Dan still staring at the Glyphs.

"He can not hear us Eric."

"If you knew about this place why didn't you tell me?" I asked slightly annoyed.

"I am here now, Eric. You need very little help from me. The upper right corner is your key. Enjoy my friend and share as I know you will."

The kings voice faded and I no longer felt his presence.

"Do you think you can open the door." said Dan with anxious eyes.

His voice pulled me back to reality.

"**I**'ll give it a good try." I answered. Why I was not telling Dan about the king's presence I had no idea.

Approaching the door I ran my fingers gently along the upper edge as I had seen Carlos do countless times. I reached the upper right corner and could feel a slight indent, a soft curve, if you will, that fit the tips of two fingers. With almost no pressure the groove edged downward and as it did the door angled open on a center pivot. There was a small rush of stale air we were able to avoid. Eventually turning back to the door Dan held the lantern up high. At first I couldn't believe my eyes. I thought I was back in the kings tomb in the lost city. I was staring at a painted mural not dissimilar to the ones in the mural corridor of the tomb. I grabbed the lantern from Dan and hurried to the painting.

*"**T**his had to be done by the same artist."* I thought.

As the others, it depicted a moment in history. Ancient history. It showed the desert and sandstone monuments, a little less wind sculpted, with two figures. One un-mistakenly Maya, the other obviously early native American, possibly Anasazi, or in other words the Ancient Ones.

Next to each was a small pile of colored stones. Blue turquoise by the native American and green jade by the Mayan. Each man had their hands extended, raised upward slightly as if a welcoming gesture.

This lone painting matched perfectly the artwork in the mural hallway of the kings tomb.

As hypnotized as I was by the realistic scene, Dan's comments drew me back to his world. Begrudgingly I tore myself away from the painting. No wonder Dan was sounding comments. We were inside an ancient museum. Clothing, and artifacts from both peoples were on display. Not a display as in a modern museum, but as if this had been an everyday working room. The ancient miners possibly resided here.

One particular tool captured my attention as it did Dan's. It was a small hand sized pick ax. We assumed it was for the final phases of chipping out the finer turquoise from its host rock. It's wonderment was not its use, but its makeup. It looked like a steel alloy which seemed impossible for it's time period. Or was it. Recalling some of the king's stories I relayed to Dan how much further advanced the king seemed to be. They possessed technology far beyond our own, even though it was not employed by all.

Dan climbed the crude steps to retrieve the generator powered lights. It was not long when the full beauty of the room was revealed.

Naturally I went camera crazy again, documenting every nook and cranny and artifact.

I finished my camera work allowing my mind to wander.

"There must be more to this room than just storage or living quarters." I thought. *"It doesn't make sense to go through this much security just to house a few artifacts."*

I looked at Dan who also appeared to be contemplating something. He caught my glance and smiled.

"**A**re you thinking what I'm thinking ?" he asked.

"**A**pparently so." I replied.

"**A**ll this secrecy just to store a few goodies ?" questioned Dan.

"**I** had the same thought just now." I offered. "But what are we looking for ?"

"**S**omething worth all this effort to hide." Dan said blandly as if thinking out loud.

I remembered the secret treasure room back at the lost city and as earlier filled Dan in on the story including the toll it took on Frank.

We continued our closer inspection of each and every item, each offering our own comments. As I neared the back wall there was a bench which held some, what I assumed to be , ceremonial outfits, both Mayan and Native American. On closer study I noticed a large earthen pot with a lid, on the floor under the bench partially hidden by the drape of the costumes.

My curiosity hasn't lead me into trouble yet so I reached for the jar and sat on the bench while opening the lid. The lid was more secure then I expected but with some extra effort it was finally freed. My verbal "OMPF'S " caught the attention of Dan who wandered over. He watched patiently as I reached inside. To my great surprise my hand touched something familiar. I gazed up at Dan and he smiled as he read the expression on my face.

"**W**hat's making you so happy?" he inquired.

I had not removed my hand yet but answered.

"**I**f this is what I think it is, we are going to celebrate tonight."

By now Dan had caught my excitement. I pulled my arm out slowly my hand gently clutching a familiar material. I was right. I was again touching an ancient scroll.

"**H**ow did you know ?" asked Lone Buffalo.

I broke into my story telling mode again describing to Dan the scroll library belonging to the king. He was beginning to like my stories.

My hands were actually shaking as I unrolled the delicate looking material. It's looks were deceiving though. It was just as sturdy as the ones I worked with in the jungle. The script was exactly the same. Of course I could not read it but the fact that it was here in the American southwest was startling news in itself. Dan, rather sheepishly asked if he could touch it.

"Look at it all you want my friend. It could be part of your history too."

He handled it like crystal glass as I did on my first introduction.

While Dan was caught up in the scroll I turned my attention again to the earthenware. I felt other articles and retrieved another roll although material wise felt different. It was a tanned hide of some sort, very thin but obviously strong. I unrolled it and once again my heart stopped while my head started to spin. Could this really be a star chart ? In my countless hours of research I had often come across various theorizing of star constellations being duplicated on the ground by ancient peoples around the globe. Even with my extremely limited knowledge of astronomy I recognized the Orion constellation. I was about to call Dan but he was already looking over my shoulder. He started with a low soft whistle then spoke quietly.

"There are some traditional oral tales of such a thing but I have never been witness to it's reality."

Dan helped me unroll the complete hide and add some weighted objects to hold it in place. We remained silent just staring at the sky on the floor. I did not know what to think. This was something never mentioned by the king.

I also had read of ancient peoples and their connection with the sun and stars worldwide . The solstice, both winter and summer, was used for planning of planting and harvesting. What I was viewing now was entirely different. This was an actual study of the heavens. Obviously, I was surmising, some advanced knowledge for use in ceremonial or religious practices.

There were markings or symbols by each star of the constellation. I could tell Dan was already working on decipherment in his mind. He looked at me uttering;

"I will need help from the elders on this one."

We studied as much as we could for fifteen minutes or so then carefully re-rolled the hide and set it aside temporarily while I reached for another item from the jar. Again it was a scroll but once more of a different material. A paper of a sort, like a papyrus I guess. Compared to the animal hide this was very fragile. Our curiosity building we both were smiling as we gently unrolled it. A great surprise for a third time now faced us. We gazed at relatively well done sketches of Mayan step pyramids next to, what really shocked us, obvious Egyptian pyramids. Further unrolling revealed pyramid shaped earthen mounds as seen in other parts of both Europe and the U.S..

As you know Eric, we tried to share our knowledge with the world."

I was so taken aback by the sudden sound of Atol's voice that I dropped my edge of the scroll. It remained dangling in the safety of Dan's hands. I was physically shaken and leaned back to catch my breath.

I did not mean to startle you, my young friend. I wanted to reaffirm what knowledge I imparted to you over the last two years."

"You could do it a little more quietly or with some sort of warning." I scolded, showing my annoyance.

"I suppose you are correct, Eric. I will heed your council in the future."

"Are you alright." inquired Dan's soft voice.

I looked up at him rather embarrassed,

"Yes, I'm fine. I guess it's all the excitement. I'll be alright in a few seconds."

"It was the King, wasn't it." Lone Buffalo asked.

Further embarrassed I admitted it was. I then went on to explain my earlier conversation with the king apologizing for having kept it a secret.

Dan, without being upset, accepted my meager apology smiling.

"There is a lot more to this advanced knowledge that I'm thinking now should be shared with the elders." I commented.

" I agree my friend but for now let's get back to the

drawings," returned Dan followed by his always warming smile.

Refocusing on the papyrus we were viewing three types of pyramids from supposedly three different time periods collectively in one location. Yet our current organized academic teachings say this is not possible.

Looking at each other, both elated and confused at our discovery I said;

"There's more in the jar."

Dan's childish enthusiasm showed as he replied;

"Well what are you waiting for ?"

My hand entered the darkness of the jar pulling out another scroll, again of papyrus but slightly smaller. Without hesitation this time I immediately opened it. We were viewing the constellation Orion again, only this time in relation to the Egyptian pyramids.

Without thinking I said out loud;

"No one is ever going to believe this or even think about accepting this."

Dan joined right in.

"But there are two of us as witnesses, from two different disciplines."

I immediately countered with;

"And hundreds out there who are going to laugh."

Lone Buffalo turned instantly serious.

"Then we'll just have to convince them."

Attempting to break our downed mood I offered.

"There's still one more scroll in the jar."

"Might as well reveal all." Dan said half heartedly.

Out came the rolled document, a material much different than the others. Unidentifiable to either of us. We slowly unrolled the fabric like material and were astonished for a fourth time as a world map came into view. Not only did it appear accurate but there were faint dotted and dashed lines between various continents with an unknown script identifying each line. This we knew would take much study.

We took a water break and while sitting just gazed around this room of history. We remained silent, each trying to justify this sudden rush of information. What does it mean ? Where was it from ? Who was it from ? How long ago was it put here ? What do we do with it ?

Chapter   14

I suddenly remembered the next obvious step. **My Camera!** Photographically recording everything in situ was absolutely necessary. Not that the academic establishment was going to accept our story but I recorded it anyway. This was proper procedure. Dan was most helpful with the various scrolls. As he said this was all part of his history and he wanted to be part of it. The lighting setup was not the best but it served its purpose for now.

Dan was looking about at the clothing outfits while I carefully rolled up the scrolls and returned them to the earthen jar.

"You have done well, Eric. Your search is almost over."

Startled yet again, I answered;

*"**S**earch ? What search ? I didn't know I was searching for anything."*

There was no answer.

*"**W**hy must you always make a mystery of everything ?"* I tried. There was still no answer. I continued to put away the scrolls thinking,

*"**W**hy am I so angry with the king lately ?" I usually want to talk to the king. I wish I knew what was bugging me."*

Luckily Dan was busy elsewhere and did not notice my preoccupation. I slid the jar back under the bench and just sat there trying to make sense of the kings words.

"Okay, what am I searching for." I mumbled in a whisper. "We found the pyramid, we found the mine shaft, we found the turquoise room, we found this hidden room."

The only next logical thing is that there must be something else yet hidden. Most likely in this room. I let Dan in on what I was just thinking and we both started an in depth recheck of the room. I even went so far as to check the entrance passageway again. That proved to be a negative so back to the trophy room I went. About a third of the way into the room, Dan called for me to stop.

"What's wrong ?" I exclaimed questioningly.

"Probably nothing, but back up a few steps." he directed.

I did as requested feeling confused.

"There! Stop there." Dan ordered, his voice raised a little. "Did you hear that ?"

Still confused I answered, "Hear what ?"

Lone Buffalo smiled sensing my quandary.

"It sounded like a hollow in the floor, or a loose board."

"Loose board ?" I thought to myself. "How can there be a loose board ? the floor is packed dirt."

I moved back and forth over a two plus foot area. Sure enough it sounded like a loose board.

Dan joined me on hands and knees as we methodically checked that particular floor area. A straight line of cracked dirt showed about a foot long. We looked at each other and smiled. Dan took out a pocket knife and began gently scrapping at the dirt. I joined him with my own knife.

Ten minutes of careful digging exposed a wooden panel approximately twenty inches square. We sat back, our usual excitement showing. I was first to break the silence.

"Your turn."

The message was clear and he immediately went to work with his knife trying to pry open the panel. It was not as easy as it looked, so I joined in. After much struggling and getting nowhere we gave up temporarily.

"You knew it wouldn't open, that's why you let me go first." quipped Dan through his always big smile.

"Of course I did, I'm no fool." I joked back.

We moved the lighting closer and proceeded to meticulously brush and blow the dirt away and off the panel. It was then we discovered minute scratch marks on the opposite ends of the two outside boards of the three board panel. Still smiling we lifted the center board, with some difficulty, and turned it toward the scratches. Sure enough it was a locking mechanism. At about forty five degrees we could hear a click and the panel was loose in our hands. After setting it aside we turned to look at the secret cache.

The repository was about eighteen inches deep and generously lined with red and gold silk. It appeared to be oriental silk. Another mystery. Cushioned in the generous folds of this rare silk was what appeared to be a large book. We guessed it to be approximately fifteen by twenty inches. Together we carefully lifted it out of its place of honor. It was not bound like any books we were familiar with. It appeared to be hand sewn with a very fine silver thread or wire. It was done with meticulous precision. It, in itself, was a work of art.

The front and back covers were of an unknown material, sturdy but light. The multi colored design work on both panels reminded me of the art of the Book of Kells.

We hesitated, prolonging the suspense.

"Your turn." I repeated to Lone Buffalo.

He nodded as he reached for the beautifully adorned cover. With a gentle touch he turned away the top art work to expose the first page. There were four Glyphs, unreadable of course, surrounded by more multi colored lines swirling around the page edges.

The paper also appeared to be of unknown material. The second page, filled with a script neither of us had ever seen, obviously was a story form or information format. We turned more pages still amazed by the colored art work. Every now and then a drawing or diagram was displayed, all beyond our understanding. Toward the middle we paused at a diagram we did recognize. The constellation Orion was again making its presence known.

This time each star was identified with a particular ancient ruin. Dwellings of the ancestors of the Navaho and Hopi, "The Ancient Ones." There were four individual pages devoted to the Star group and its corresponding ancient dwelling on the earth.

The latter part of this magnificent treasure appeared to represent cultures from all over the globe, their script, Glyphs and even drawn representations of buildings and animals.

After closing the book we sat there speechless. Would anybody ever believe this. I had my doubts. By the king's own admission his teachings for thousands of years went unheeded and un-believed. What do I, a mere nobody, do with this information ? I put forth my thoughts to Lone Buffalo who admitted he was perplexed as I was..

On a more positive note Dan agreed to set up a meeting with the elders as soon as practical. We agreed the book should stay here for now as it has for who knows how many centuries. Perhaps even longer.

We still had plenty of daylight left but decided to call it quits. We have had enough excitement and surprises for one day. We parted on a high note congratulating each other on the discoveries of the day.

On the way to my motel I stopped for some Italian take away and some cold beer. I just wanted to vege out tonight. I might even spoil myself and watch a little television to hopefully clear my mind.

The food wasn't too bad, the beer was at least cold and leave it to my luck the only movie on the TV was "Raiders of the Lost Ark" Just what I didn't need. I turned off the set and sat outside enjoying the sunset with a cold beer. The stars began to show themselves but the last thing I wanted to look at tonight was constellations. I returned to my darkened room and to bed

Chapter   15

Sleep was not easily forthcoming. At first I couldn't get to sleep with thoughts of the book and its meaning racing through my mind. When I did doze off dreams permeated my subconscious with all sorts of weird connections of the ancient global world. Exhaustion finally took over in the wee hours and I awoke with the sun in my eyes. MY clock shouted eight forty five and I quickly jumped out of bed, suddenly remembering there was no rush.

I was awaiting a call from Lone Buffalo. I decided a shower was in order to hopefully rinse away the cobwebs from my lack of sleep. I enjoyed a leisurely breakfast thinking of the mysterious book.

Atal's name came to mind so I tried to call him. I shifted my thoughts from the book to the king.

"I am here my friend. I am glad to see you are no longer angry with me. I truly did not mean to upset you."

"Forgive me my friend. I had no reason to be cross with you." I answered.

Before I could continue the king spoke out.

"You summoned me because you have questions about the book. Am I correct Eric ?"

"Yes, I was curious...." As usual I was cut off.

"You were curious about its age, its contents and how to interpret it. Am I correct ?"

Again he answered his own question.

"Of* course *you are. That is what I like about you, always eager to learn."

This time it was my turn to interrupt.
"Will you help me ? I feel this is a knowledge the whole world should know about."

"You are absolutely correct Eric. I wish you luck. Perhaps you can succeed where I have failed. But I think you will find, as I, the minds of today, as always, are not willing to accept what may be beneficial to them. Established thinking does not like to be criticized or proven wrong. Closed minds are the norm it seems."

"I can not disagree with your assessment, but will you help me ?" I asked, almost pleadingly.

"I will give you a start my young friend. I believe you are resourceful enough to make your own conclusions."

He paused as if to let me speak. I remained silent.

"You are looking at the world's history at that point in time."

The kings voice began to trail off. I knew the signal. I asked anyway.
"What date would that be ?"
As I suspected, we no longer were connected. I was alone with my silence.
I realized had I gained nothing from the king. The fact that it was a history I'm sure I could have figured out. Oh well, let's hope the elders can shed some light. Note to self: Call Mario.
I daydreamed away a few hours trying not to think of the

-The Ancient Ones-

book.

   Just after eleven Dan Called. A meeting was set up with the elders for one this afternoon. Now I was excited again. Making sure I was presentable I drove to the school.

   I arrived a little early so Dan and I could share some thoughts together. He explained a few hints to the elders in order to get the meeting but wanted me to make the presentation. Now, still excited, but I also felt a tinge of nervousness. I hoped I wouldn't make a fool of myself. Dan, sensing my quandary spoke quietly;

   I'm with you all the way Pal. We either sink or swim together."

   Surprisingly this made me feel better. I smiled confidently. "Okay, let's do it."

   We met in the same hall as before, this time there was an additional member with the elders. He was truly an elder. It's hard to tell with Native American's but I guessed him to be in his nineties. I did find out later he was ninety seven.

   I felt as if I were on stage with ten pair of eyes on me and not a single smile among them. I made up my mind to start from the beginning, why I was here and the like, even my connection with the Maya. All eyes stayed fixed on me. Periodically I glanced over to Lone Buffalo and received an affirmative nod. I was surprised at myself but it did add confidence and bolster my spirt. I now felt right in what I was doing.

   I told my complete story in detail. I even mentioned the blue tarantula. Amazingly enough, my attention to my furry friend caught the interest of the elders. It gave me credibility.

   According to the elders, especially the ninety seven year old, they explained that one who can freely communicate with other creatures from the Great Spirit possesses an inner quality and communion with the unknown spirit world. Only chosen ones can perform these feats. There were now expressions of sincere interest and knowing smiles of approval. They urged me to continue my story.

   A warmth filled my being as if I were suddenly accepted. I could feel more enthusiasm in my story telling. The nods and smiles told me my tale was being accepted.

   I completed my story of discovery with as much detail as I

could muster. The last days revelation of the Book piqued everyones interest. My story completed I sat back awaiting reactions.

The newly arrived senior elder spoke only in the language of the Navajo. He spoke slowly and deliberately for two or three minutes the whole while looking at me. When he became silent the others translated for me what he had said. They told me his name was Whispering Wind. I was to find out later that Lone Buffalo knew of him but never met him.

Whispering Wind remembered being told of a special book from the Great Spirit that recorded history of the Ancients. Of special dwelling places of lost peoples who were advanced beyond the Navajo way of life. Peoples who had art, music & knowledge of the stars. They had pointed structures that were temples to the gods. They collected and worked gemstones for their beauty, also gold, silver and platinum. They performed feats of medicine and surgery that could rival today's advanced skills. They are all gone now. The greed of the old world explorers destroyed these advanced cultures for nothing but the riches of gold and silver. They destroyed a culture that was beyond their comprehension.

Hearing these words of Whispering Wind was like an echo of the king. I was humbled to be in his presence.

The elders dismissed both Dan and I. My words would be discussed and we would be summoned after they reached their decision. As we were leaving Whispering Wind signaled my attention. He grasped my hand in both of his.

"Do not ever ignore the silence of the Great Spirits other creatures. We can learn much from them. Their wisdom can be of a great council to us if we choose to listen."

The touch of his hands seemed to impart a living connection to the Ancients in me. An unknowing, indescribable tingle zapped through my body.

Once outside the meeting room Dan with his usual big smile said.

"You made quite an impression in there. They don't take to outsiders very easily."

Although my visit was temporarily over it was now that I started to become nervous.

"How long do you think they will take ?" I asked Dan.

"No telling" was his answer. I actually have not had too many dealings with the elders. The visit I had with you before this was only my second. I have never had reason to be here before."

Less then thirty minutes had passed when the pair were recalled by the elders. The looks I now received did not make me feel comfortable. I believe Dan felt it also because of the questioning quick look he gave me. We sat at the far end of the table and remained silent.

Talking silently among themselves a word I did not understand was mentioned a few times. "Baa Nahashneii and Weshnihi. I turned to Dan for an explanation. He appeared to be a little embarrassed but did answer quietly.

"Roughly translated it means "Story Teller" and not necessarily factual."

At first his words hit me like a club, but gathering my composure I tried to hide my disappointment as best I could.

Now speaking English I was advised it was a very good story but a book as I described was a bit of a stretch for the imagination.

At this Dan jumped up and spoke out excitedly and instantly.

"But it is true, I was there with him. I saw it, I touched it. You must see for yourself."

Calm down Lone Buffalo, let us finish our proposal." said Dove of Spring.

Quietly sitting back Dan bowed his head to their authority. The woman continued looking directly at me and speaking slowly and distinctly;

"However, we are willing to see for ourselves. Apparently you made a very good impression with Whispering Wind and because of his influence you have won the day."

I suddenly felt alive again.

"As our senior elder we value his council. He has felt the truth of what you said. Give us some time and we will meet you at this mine. Let's say about three o'clock."

"Thank you." I said smiling gratefully. "I promise you will not be disappointed."

"We shall see." commented Dove of Spring cautiously.

Dan also thanked them but in his Native tongue.

We left with high spirits.

Going directly to the pyramid we waited, choosing not to

un-tarp anything just yet. As promised at three P.M. a van showed up carrying nine of the ten elders. My wish was answered when I saw Whispering Wind was among them. When all were in position to witness, Dan and I swung aside the tarp's covering the pyramid and its entrance. The elders were silent as they gazed in awe at the pyramid structure in their desert.

Dan entered first but not before pointing out my furry blue friend perched on the door lintel for all to see. Whispering Wind just smiled nodding his head in an affirmative manner.

Dan continued on into the pyramid starting the generator making sure the lights were up and running. The elders were occupied with studying the structure exterior. Their words were all in their Native language way beyond my comprehension.

Reappearing, Dan urged the elders inside explaining the details as he went. Two by two they descended to the lower interior. They had just entered the turquoise room as I joined them. I took them to where we found the bodies of the miners, both Navajo and Mayan.

This distinguished group were all used to turquoise but never this high quality and so much of it. Whispering Wind would say a few words every now and then capturing the instant attention of the others. You could tell he still held command.

"The Book ?" asked Dove of Spring quietly, looking directly at me non expressive.

Dan and I smiled at each other as we moved to the large pile of blue stone. To the amazement of our guests we removed the large panels revealing the stair well. I watched carefully as expressions changed. Their "Weshnihi" name for me might have been premature.

Single file we all proceeded to the lower level. Fascinated by the mini museum the elders moved about slowly taking in every detail. The periodic utterances of our ninety seven year old special guest were answered with accepting nods.

Repeating herself, Dove of Spring asked about the book.

"This presentation is all yours my friend. This is yours to prove." remarked Dan.

Without hesitation I advanced to the floor panel removing the boards. There for all to see, enveloped by the rare oriental silks was "The Book". I started to reach for it when I felt a hand on my shoulder. It was Whispering Wind and he was saying something. Dan translated;

"He wants you to step away for a moment."

-The Ancient Ones-

I did as requested observing the Old Man taking some herb like substance from a medicine pouch attached to his waist. Sprinkling some on the Book he began a low guttural chant, answered in turn by the others. This lasted for a minute or so. I was then instructed to retrieve "The Book". Once in my possession I handed it to Whispering Wind who in turn treated it like fragile glass. He stared at the cover, softly smiling, again nodding his head up and down. He mumbled a few incoherent words and then authoritatively spoke to the others which Dan quietly translated for me.

*"**T**his is the fulfillment of what I was told as a child by my great grandfather, who in turn was told by his grandfather and so passed on since the Great Spirit was but a boy. This is an accounting of all of the ancients actions. From beyond the rising sun to beyond the setting sun, for as long as there have been stars. This tell us of ourselves and our brethren whom we have never met from parts of our world we have never seen. We all are as of one, as it should be, yet there are those few who would wantonly destroy the very fabric of peaceful coexistence, turned by their individual need to possess something that is not theirs."*

Here the wise old sage paused, turned to me, smiled, and struggling with the English words said;

*"**Y**ou have done well my Son. The Great Spirit is pleased."*

Turning to the other elders and his native tongue ;

*"**T**onight we shall feast and I will read of the Ancients, our past and our future."*

Silence prevailed as "The Book" was passed to each of the elders as each recited a prayer in Navajo. "The Book having made its rounds finally returned to Whispering Wind, he directed Dan to retrieve the rare silks which he reverently wrapped and secured around "The Book". With a humble smile he presented it to me.

The elders, in turn bowed to me and "The Book" as they passed by to return to the upper world. I stood there dumbfounded as each passed. Lone Buffalo stood proudly by sporting his usual half smile.

The van drove off with "The Book" leaving Dan and I alone in the desert. We chose not to speak for quite a while and were joined by Mr. Blue, who also remained still and silent.

I had mixed emotions about "The Book" leaving my, or should I say our, possession. Our cursory scan was only enough to whet our appetite. It appeared Dan felt the same as I based on what he said to me.

"They will revere and take care of "The Book", Eric. They also are aware of what it means to both of us and the work we went through to recover it. I have no doubts that we will be able to study it."

"I want to photograph it, for its protection, it must be preserved, then we can study it in detail."

"Whispering Wind has obviously taken a liking to you. The other elders will not go against him."

"I hope you're right." I answered.

As if that quandary was settled Mr. Blue turned away from us and wandered into the desert.

It was shortly after five and the late afternoon sun was beginning its magic show of color as it played with the desert sands and sandstone sentinels. This show as always can brighten up anyone's day. Dan suggested a quiet dinner before we parted for the night. We spoiled ourselves at a fine steak house accompanied by a good bottle of wine. It was just about ten P.M. when I arrived at my humble rooms feeling quite relaxed. The bed embraced me warmly as I entered dream land.

Chapter 16

I answered the telephone on the fourth ring still half asleep. It was a bright and cheerful Lone Buffalo. Arrangements had been made for me to photograph "The Book" that afternoon just after one o'clock. In the meantime Dan planned for his class to visit the now open mine. I agreed to meet him there. After all these kids deserved to see the results of their digging efforts. It would be a nice reward to have a look back at their history.

The morning went well with the young ones and I was glad to be heading back to the school and "The Book". All the necessary equipment was in my car and I was truly anxious to get started. Upon arrival at the school Dan informed me that he took the liberty of loaning my journal of my time in the Yucatan to the elders. Surprised but not upset I asked why.

"To prove your credibility." he said. "To the elders that you are a serious scientist and not a treasure hunter."

I smiled at this, having never considered myself a scientist.

A building, separate from where we met before, was now housing "The Book". Dove of Spring and Whispering Wind were the only two to meet us there. Dove of Spring was the first to speak.

"My apologies, Mr. Dexter, for my doubts about your sincerity. Lone Buffalo has shared some of your past with us and I now admit we misjudged you and your quest. You have given us some history we could only have dreamed of. Our celebration feast has not yet taken place. Such happenings are for tribal members only. We elders are asking you to attend because of what you have given us. Lone Buffalo will keep you informed on this matter. We are in your debt."

As before, Dan stood by, proudly smiling.

Feeling humbled but pleased I returned;

"No apology necessary. I would have doubted me also had our positions been reversed."

When Dove of Spring moved away I looked inquiringly at him.

"That was not my doing. I said nothing to the elders." he exclaimed.

Whispering Wind took my hand in both of his again and that same tingle filled my body. He did not utter a word but I heard him say:

"I think I know your king."

I could detect a smile with his eyes as he knew I received his message. Neither of us showed an outward sign of what just transpired. He then led us to the "The Book", spoke a few words to Lone Buffalo and left the room. Dan repeated his words in English for me.

"Let me know when you are finished. We will lock up."

After photographing all those scrolls in the Yucatan this was short work. Dan was of great help. I was satisfied with my results and within two hours we were packing up. Dan reported our completion while I returned my equipment to the car.

With plenty of daylight left we decided to go back to the desert pyramid. Once again viewing the vault of "The Book", we further searched for other objects. Not expecting to find any, we were disappointed anyway. Returning to the museum level we performed a second search thorough of both floor and walls. We found no niches or trap doors of any kind. We convinced each other of our thoroughness because Mr. Blue was nowhere to be seen. We repeated our checking of the other three walls only to find they were solid and hid nothing.

Feeling our day was complete we closed up the various rooms and sealed off the pyramid as best we could. Dan went back to the school while I sat soaking up the beauty of the desert. Before long I was joined by Mr, Blue.

"What do you think my friend, will "The Book" tell us anything."

Two of his legs twitched as if he was answering. I remembered Whispering Winds words. He believed in the wisdom of the other creatures of the Great Spirit. Who am I to go against such ancient teachings. Perhaps Mr. Blue was trying to communicate.

"Was that it Mr. Blue ? Were you trying to tell me something ? If so, what ?"

My tarantula friend again moved the same two legs.

I sort of laughed at myself. My friends back east, who are not adventurous, will really think I'm crazy. First I talk to the ancient dead and
now I'm communicating with spiders. I guess the rocks will be next. On a more practical note, if the rocks could talk I'm sure they could tell us a lot about history.

I stayed in the desert till almost dark. I guess I was just soul searching, thinking of the last few days events, thinking of the last few years of my life. How lucky I was to have experienced what I did. How confused I was as to why me being privy to such happenings.

The sun was saying its last farewell when I decided to go home. I said my goodbyes to Mr. Blue who immediately turned and vanished into the shadows. Something light to eat was in order to end this curious day.

Chapter 17

I almost forgot what brought me to "The Book". My shadowed lines to nowhere sure evolved to a whole new scenario of events I was not prepared for. I wasn't sorry for what transpired. I just felt temporarily lost. Where do I go from here ? True, I was looking forward to the readings and study of "The Book" but in the meantime I craved something more tangible or physical.

Perhaps that's it, I told myself. I made up my mind then and there to go back to the desert before sunrise tomorrow, camera ready and look for more shadow lines.

For whatever reason this truly fascinated me. In addition, the jungle had its distinctive music while here I have the ever changing color palette of some of the worlds best art. Just the thought of such a change of venue back to my original quest rejuvenated my spirit. Before lights out I called Dan and left a message of my intended plans and that I would call him later that day.

~ ~ ~

I could feel the excitement building as I drove to the desert. I bypassed the pyramid area heading for one of the wind sculptures I saw from the site. I parked the car and sat with my back to the tall sandstone cliff patiently awaiting the sun. While waiting my thoughts went to Mr. Blue. "No need for that." I said aloud. "He's at least five or six miles away." I scolded myself for being silly when I saw the first golden ray break the eastern horizon.

"Show me something." I pleaded aloud.

The sun crept ever so slowly as if it were teasing me. As I stood there my wish was fulfilled. Two very faint lines appeared again about twenty five feet apart. I followed with my eyes as it continued as far as I could see. The start or end depending on how you wanted to look at it, was approximately twenty odd feet from the tall sandstone cliff.. I was so puzzled by this fact that I clearly forgot to take any photos. When my head cleared the lines had vanished.

"You blew it again Eric." I laughed out loud

I wasn't upset though. My inquisitive mind took over. If this was a roadway of sorts, where was it going ? Why did it end at the bottom of this cliff ,which I judged to be at least two hundred feet high. ? There were no outward signs of a perpendicular road intersecting this one. It would be difficult to detect by shadow lines because of the sun angle in relation to the sandstone mountain.

I gave myself a water break to sit and contemplate this current quandary. Was there something special about this particular rock mass ? I looked up and determined this was next to impossible to climb, at least for me anyway. I decided perhaps I should look more closely at this mini mountain. I glanced both right and left to see the challenge before me. I approximated it to be four hundred plus yards long. Oh well, what else do I have to do.

I set off to my left following the sheer cliff, taking in every detail I could. I did not expect to see anything exceptional considering the desert winds constantly reshaping the sandstone for hundreds and even thousands of years.

Every now and then I thought I detected something odd. The only thing odd was letting my imagination carry me away. An hour or so later found me at the west end. I guessed about another one hundred yards would bring me to the north side. I marveled at natures work sculpting these silent sentinels. I let my mind wander trying to imagine what the area looked like a few thousand years ago.

Rounding this misshapen mountain, I headed East. This side, I guess because of the wind changes, showed a different pattern of lines like the grain of wood. Each side of this mystical mountain had designs unique to themselves.

Though the slopes on the north side were less steep they were still beyond my ability to climb. Another two and a half hours found me back where I started having observed nothing I would consider out of the ordinary. *"A reminder to myself to check the aerial photos tonight to see if I could detect anything on the mountain top."*

I sat down to rest still slightly confused. Why have a road suddenly end at a steep mountain ? Perhaps this wasn't even a roadway.

Maybe the shadow lines I saw were just a freak wind formation. Feeling a bit down I lay back, my hands behind my head staring at the ever blue sky. I must have been tired and dozed off because I awoke with a start from a dream. I wouldn't call it a nightmare or even a bad dream. It was like an idea that just popped into my head.

Hundreds of years ago this hunk of rock would have been taller and wider. Who knows how many feet wider. That would put the end of the road closer to the mountain. Perhaps close to an entrance.

I laughed at myself again.

"There you go Eric, letting wishful thinking control you. Oh , what the hell, I'm already here."

I struggled to my feet and checked where I thought I saw the end of the shadow lines. Standing facing the cliff I looked around. Obviously, there would be no entrance into the mountain because of the many centuries erosion. That only leaves down. On a whim I grabbed a short piece of rebar from the car and started poking the desert floor. As I suspected, just loose dirt and sand. I moved closer to the mountain while I continued to poke.

"Thud"

I said ouch out loud as the sudden thud reverberated through my hand and wrist. Now on my knees, I started digging. Down I went. When I seriously scraped my knuckles, enough to draw blood, I wished I had my shovel. I wrapped my kerchief around my two fingers and continued to dig. I soon hit my goal. It was just a large piece of rough edged sandstone. Bigger than I could lift. I poked around some more and had many more "thuds". I guessed a chunk must have fallen off the steep rise and eventually was buried by the ever moving sands. As a matter of curiosity I poked around some more and again hit something solid. This time the sound and feel was totally different. Just from experience it felt like hitting wood. Unfortunately it was deeper than and under the chunk of sandstone. I quit for the day then and there. I drove back to the motel hoping Dan would be available with his backhoe.

Lone Buffalo answered the phone right away, curious as to where I had been all day. I related my story to him and of course he was interested right away. We made plans for the next day. I was to meet him bright and early at the pyramid, then head for my latest puzzle.

~ ~ ~

Seven thirty A.M. saw us both at the mine site. Dan questioned me right away with his usual bright smile.

"Where do you get your luck from ? He asked. "I've been walking this desert since I was a kid and other than a stray piece of turquoise now and then I have found absolutely nothing."

Laughing I answered;

"You're problem is that you don't talk to tarantulas though I must admit he did not lead me to this, if it even is anything."

Laughing with me now Dan said;

"Okay Pal, let's move out. Lead the way but not too fast. This backhoe is a slow mover."

We made it to the site in question with Dan still looking puzzled.

"There's nothing here." He was stating the obvious.

"It may look that way but I still want to dig here." I explained as I pointed to the place I detected the thuds.

"Okay Eric, but I think you're wasting your time. What could be here ? This was probably once covered by the missing pieces of this sandstone mountain, who knows how many centuries ago."

Lone Buffalo moved his machine into position as I directed and lowered the bucket for his first scoop. Luck was with us, he was able to capture my knuckle scraping remnant on his first try. He moved it back and out of the way as I peered into the vacancy it left. Sand was slowly sifting into the hole but I saw no wood. I grabbed a three foot piece of rebar and pressed slowly. My weird sounding "THUD" happened again. It was quite deep. I had Dan take shallower bites with the backhoe. Finally exposed were finely hewn logs, and as other times it was wood I did not recognize. I indicated to Dan to stop his machine and join me with a shovel.

We hand dug but were making absolutely no progress. The sand in this area was extremely loose and was filling in the hole faster than we could throw it out.

Returning to the backhoe Dan began clearing a larger circumference around the logs. Even this was slow going due to the fineness of the sand. Almost a half hour went by when we agreed the area should now be large enough. We were both tired now yet anxious to see more of these buried logs. Slowly we dug around them moving dirt and sand to the now cleared area.

The logs turned out to be ten feet long by one foot wide

precisely fitted together, tied together at both ends with hide strapping. As a unit we could not move them. Choosing not to undo the strapping we returned to the backhoe. Dan as gently as he could was able to lift the mass from the middle of one side.   Slowly it raised to show a shaft heading deep underground. We left the backhoe in place to hold up the log platform rather than have it slip on us. Being careful of the loose sand we stepped to the edge to look down. It was rather deep and dark but a ladder was permanently affixed to one side. It looked strong but as a precaution we retrieved some rope from my car along with the lantern. With the rope secured around my waste I dared the ladder. The shaft was lined with boards and was quite solid with the ladder attached with what looked like nails. The nail heads being rather large and angle shaped.

       I descended slowly, one step at a time. I could not believe how sturdy all seemed to be. The lantern showed no end in sight. If it wasn't for echo I would not have heard Dan calling to me. It was obvious he was concerned for my safety. Thoughts were racing through my mind as to how this was built and by whom. Every now and then I thought I could make out scratching's on the shaft wall. If it was script or hieroglyphics they were too faint to read. I wouldn't have understood them anyway since translations were not my thing.

       Down and down I went, resting every now and then. The air was becoming stale so I rested for five minutes or so hoping the air from above would finally filter down, which it did. It just took longer then I expected.

       Somewhat refreshed I resumed my downward trek. The lantern finally showed a floor. The walls at the bottom flared out somewhat boxing a space about ten by ten feet. This flare out was also boarded for safety sake I guess. It was no use calling up to Lone Buffalo, I was far too deep. I methodically looked around at nothing save for a three by four foot panel of dissimilar wood on the floor near one corner. Naturally I attempted to lift it and discovered it to be extremely light. It covered a rectangular pit a touch smaller than its cover and two and a half feet deep. My eyes were instantly drawn to a magnificently designed and constructed chest. A carrying handle adorned all four sides. The wood was dark and well polished holding a variety of designs like I had never seen before. They were constructed of fine gold highlighted with silver. The corners were reenforced with both, what looked at first glance, to be iron and bronze. The outer dimensions of the chest I estimated to be two by three feet.

       On my knees I tried to open the lid. Disappointment filled my being. It was obviously locked. Naturally the next obvious thing was to try lifting. On my belly I reached for one of the handles which felt rather strong. I pulled and much to my surprise it did rise on one end. I realized though it would be much to bulky and heavy for one man, especially going up the straight walled ladder.

I sat back resting, my mind going wild with curiosity. The thoughts, coming so fast and furious I actually shook my head to make them stop. I needed a change of air and a change of scenery to come back to normal. I stepped to the ladder and started my ascent giving a few tugs on the rope alerting Dan of my return.

It took a while to reach the top and I was quite exhausted by the time I saw the sun. Dan helped me on the last few steps and also kept his inquisitiveness in check awaiting my breath to return to normal. As I started to speak he was instantly by my side encouraging my story. I don't believe I left any detail uncovered. I also did not hesitate to encourage him to make the descent to see this magnificent spectacle. I handed him my camera to record that wondrous event in situ. With the camera safely strapped around his neck he began his downward climb. Almost twenty minutes passed when I felt the rope jiggle signaling Dan's return. As his head broke the surface his broad smile was the first thing that caught my eye. I knew then he was feeling what I had felt. At that given moment there could not have been two happier people in the world. As he did with me I gave him his time to catch his breath, then listened as he repeated what I had said earlier.

"Did you get pictures." I asked.

"Of course I did. Someone has to do your job." he joked. "And you're right, that chest is too much for one man."

His confirmation of that fact was a bit of a disappointment until he added;

"But I have a winch on the backhoe that should handle it very nicely."

I had not thought of that but I was sure glad he did.

We set about making the necessary preparations . I was to go down with rope and the winch cable and prepare a sling for the chest while Dan operated the apparatus from topside. I would follow the chest up on the ladder guiding the cable so as not to have the chest swinging and hitting the sides of the shaft. Both of us knew we were taking a risk and most likely should have additional help, yet we chose to forge ahead with the project as planned.

I took to the ladder again cable and rope carefully attached to my body not wanting to drop anything on the chest that would mar it in any way. It was slow going carrying the extra weight and using both hands on the ladder. Once on the bottom I signaled my arrival and set about rigging a sling for the chest. It took a while but when finished I was confident the chest was well secured and protected. I rested a bit while giving a double check to my handy work. Satisfied I gave the signal to Dan to commence the lift. As soon as the slack was taken up and the chest was free swinging I slowly started up the ladder keeping pace. All was going well, slow but going well.

About a third of the way up things changed. The vibration of the winch motor on the backhoe caused some sand disturbance around the platform being held by the bucket claw of the backhoe. Before Dan even noticed or could react the platform, slipped away from the bucket and fell closing the shaft opening. In doing so jammed the winch cable against the top edge of the shaft opening. This in turn caused the cable to go taut slamming the chest against the ladder and me pinning me flat. I could feel a sudden sharp pain in the thigh and hip area. The taut cable and the weight of the chest had me pinned quite well. Immediate movement ceased. My left arm was squashed against the ladder step indicated also by a sudden pain.

I found out later that Dan, topside, tried to yell a warning but to no avail. In actuality, he fared no better. The movement of the wooden pallet happened so fast he could not get out of the way. As the cable stiffened itself against the machine it threw him off balance, The cable pinned him against the backhoe allowing his foot to be trapped under the weight of the platform as it hit the ground.

I still had one free arm and managed to switch on the lantern hanging from my belt. Looking up I could no longer see daylight nor could I move the chest.

"Okay, Eric, stay calm." I told myself. "Assess the problem and work accordingly."

My trapped leg was giving me more pain which I had to overcome in order to think.

Lone Buffalo managed to reverse the winch which allowed some slack. Enough to give him some free body movement. That same slack permitted the cable to slide with the weight of the chest freeing my body. My leg began to throb with the sudden freedom as the blood rushed back to my leg.

Now free to bend, Dan used his hands to scrape away the sand and dirt eventually freeing his foot. Totally unencumbered he was free to move around, although with much discomfort. Ignoring his own pain he climbed into the seat of the backhoe. He knew he could not move the machines position because of the winch cable but did manage to maneuver the claw and again lift the platform. As luck would have it it positioned itself against the large chunk of sandstone preventing it from sliding. He lifted it high enough to allow him total access to the shaft. Locking his machine in place he rushed as best he could to the shaft opening calling my name. I heard him and answered.

After gauging each others injuries we decided to continue the chest lift.

Setting the winch on the slowest speed possible to limit the vibration we commenced the lift process. Just the thought of getting out of the dark shaft made me feel somewhat better. Ten more minutes brought me to the surface and the sun and with a helping hand from Dan I was totally out of the shaft.

The chest hung suspended and appeared to be secure so Dan and I rested while checking each others injuries. We agreed we needed medical attention but nothing of an emergent nature. The water and rest worked miracles on our spirits as we traded curiosities as to what secrets the chest contained.

Anxious to continue we slowly, with grunts and groans, made it to our feet and through some light stretching.

With careful maneuvers we brought the chest safely to solid ground and removed the strapping. The full light of the day highlighted its full beauty. This was the work of a true artisan. There was no telling of its age and we chose not to even venture a guess. Again we rested not taking our eyes from the work of art highlighted by the sun. Still speculating on the contents we loaded it in my truck and proceeded to Dan's office. With the help of others we transferred our treasure to the empty room adjacent to the office. Our curiosity would have to wait as we sought needed medical attention then a good lunch.

~ ~ ~ ~ ~

The doctors reports on both of us was favorable. Our cuts and scraps were cleansed and dressed, an the x-rays of both showed no broken bones. We would be sore and stiff for a while but no long term damage.

Smiling we exited the clinic aiming right for the cafeteria. We just made it before they shut down for the day. The cheese burger and milkshake never tasted so good.

During lunch Lone Buffalo suggested sharing our find with

the elders. I had no objection to this what so ever, after all, this was their history.

Lunch over I returned to the chest while Dan sought out the elders. Alone with this special box I inspected it carefully on all sides in awe of its beauty.

"Again you have done well, Eric

I was not surprised at all hearing the kings voice. I almost expected it

"You knew of this ?" I questioned.

"Yes Eric. It is all part of what I have been telling you of since we met. This is history others do not want to accept, yet it is there for all to see if you choose to."

"Do you know what the chest contains ?" I inquired further.

"That is your's to discover. I'm sure you will be pleased."

I suddenly felt an emptiness, an old familiar feeling. I knew I was alone again.

The chest sported a magnificent lock system. A hinged hasp built as a part of the whole, a keyhole of a design I had never witnessed before. An intricate combination of zig - zags and curves at a slight off set angle. Obviously something that would be extremely difficult to copy. The rivets or nails holding the metal hardware in place were too beautiful to consider drilling or prying open. Smiling to myself, *"We may never know what mysteries lie within."*

I sat back to relax my leg still admiring the workmanship of the Ancient Ones. Day dreaming of where the chest had been I was startled awake with the return of Dan accompanied by Dove of Spring. Others were not available at this time. Extending her hand along with a smile, Dove of Spring offered;

"I see we are indebted to you once again Mr. Dexter."

"Eric, please." I returned.

"You seem to have a knack for our history and that of the Maya from what I read of your journal."

Smiling and almost embarrassed I answered;

"Just beginners luck, Mam"

She nodded at my answer but was already fixated on the chest. She made a motion with her hand and murmured low a few words in her native tongue. She completely circled the table repeating the special words.

"This is truly a wonderful thing. What an enlightenment this must hold. Would you mind Sir, if we moved this to the council room ? This should have our forever protection."

I must have displayed a sudden look of disappointment which Dove of Spring picked up on.

"Not to worry Mr. Dexter." Correcting herself, "Eric. Though you are not one of us, you will maintain the same privileges as the elders. Total access is yours. You have proved yourself a true friend of the "Dineh".

I was speechless and humbled. I was not here for praise. Curiosity was driving me. Finally finding words;

"You honor me, Mam, more than I deserve." I did not know what else to say.

Lone Buffalo was beaming with pride for me and Dove of Spring's smile was genuine.

"I understand you received some unwanted attention during the retrieval process. If you will come, both of you, to the council fire tonight we will attend to your recovery. I will take my leave now. I am sure Whispering Wind will be seeking you out."

Her hand touched my shoulder gently as she bowed her head ever so lightly then turned and left.

Still dumbfounded, I stood there like a jerk with my mouth hanging open. Dan brought me to reality when he said;

"See Pal, now you are as much Navajo as I am." And emphasized it with his forever smile.

~ ~ ~ ~ ~ ~

Lone Buffalo did as I had done earlier He carefully inspected the chest, top bottom and sides all the while mumbling incoherently both in Navajo and English. He was as fascinated as I was.

"You don't often see craftsmanship such as this, even today." was his comment.

I said " I agree." then furthered with "Did you notice the lock ?"

"Yes, and from the looks of it a modern lock picker will have a difficult time of it."

"If at all." I added.

"Back to our questions. What is inside ? The king gave me no real clues, or did he."

I reflected on his most recent words but still was not sure of their meaning.

Dan interrupted my thoughts.

"Do you have any ideas on how to open it ?" he quizzed.

"No" I answered. "And I sure as hell don't want to break or damage it."

"I agree on that Pal, I would rather leave it as a work of art."

We both smiled.

"Tell you what." Dan continued, "As long as we have time why don't I get a wheeled cart and we can move this to the council room."

I agreed and Dan quickly turned and left the room.

Back in five minutes with a strong steel dolly Dan and I transferred the mysterious chest to the cart and directed it to the council room. This was a separate building that, to me anyway, had a sacred air about it. Again this was for tribal members only but I was blessed with their special dispensation.

I was stunned by the beauty of its interior. This was more of what I expected. You could see the pride in their history in the finishing of the large room. Their ancient weapons, prided eagle feathers, outstanding woven blankets, sand paintings, jewelry and hides of all kinds. There was too much to take in with one initial glance. Lone Buffalo allowed me time before we permanently secured the chest. Again I felt humbled and honored to be witness to their sacred inner life.

Locating the intended spot we set the chest to rest in its place of honor. With nothing more to do until the night time council fire we returned to Dan's classroom where we relaxed and discussed the days events.

Chapter 18

Dan provided a light supper for us both prior to going to the council fire. The evening weather was decent so we walked to the event which was about a fifteen minute walk to the other side of the compound. We were not going to a modern building but all at once there before me was a traditional hogan This particular one was a large eight sided structure. I could feel myself getting all excited again. Stepping back in time as it were. Smoke was rising from a center hole, spiraling up to the Great Spirit. A heavy buffalo robe securely covered the entrance. I could not wait to get inside.

It looked even larger inside than out. There was clusters of people, both men and women scattered in small circular groups. The elders, including Whispering Wind, sat in a semi circle against the wall opposite the entranceway. This was, of course, the place of honor.

Most of those present were dressed in traditional garb. A few were a combination of modern and traditional clothes. Turquoise and silver jewelry was prominent on just about everybody. My eyes were busy soaking up this historical atmosphere.

The walls were adorned with a great variety of artifacts attesting to the peoples heritage. The center fire pit was at least ten feet in diameter. The fringe of the fire was low building up to the center of two or three feet. The draft was absolutely perfect. All smoke went straight up, there was no residue clinging inside this great hogan.

I sat on the floor with Dan, as did everyone else, to the left of the elders a quarter of the way around this massive hogan.

An almost silent drum beat was heard along with a low melodic chant. This went on for a while till finally an exquisitely costumed man entered. He danced around the fire three times sprinkling something as he circled. This caused instant flare ups accompanied by utterances from the dancer. I found out later he was the medicine man, or holy man, or shaman, and his words were a blessing.

The dancer stopped and signaled an end to the drum and

chanting. Dove of Spring spoke in her Navajo language and in turn the medicine man, "Sky above the Mountain", walked to Dan and me asking in English for us to stand. We spoke aloud before all present with a recount of the incident and the severity of our injuries. Each of us was given a medicine bundle consisting of a salve to rub on and a powder to mix with water and drink. The combinations were different for the two of us.

      Sky above the Mountain retired and Dove of Spring continued her leadership roll speaking only in her own language. On queue, Whispering Wind stood to speak. He caught my eye and with an almost imperceptible nod and smile of recognition he proceeded to tell of a long ago story of the Ancient Ones both from the North and South. This tale was his translation of "The Book". Lone Buffalo quietly interpreted him word for word. The story mentioned a great people from the South who came to them when the sun was young. He briefly recounted another tale of others appearing with the rising sun, with great teachings that made them what they are today. He talked uninterrupted for some twenty minutes holding every ones interest without question. Abruptly he sat down.

      Quiet whispering invaded the hogan and as the din increased all eyes turned to Dan and I. Dove of Spring eventually stood and with both arms raised began a monotone chant. Soon all joined her along with a back ground of soft drums. Just as suddenly she lowered her arms and all was quiet. She reseated herself as the crowd slowly filed past us and left the council fire.

      Dan and I were left alone with the elders. We received thanks from each one individually and in English, except for Whispering Wind. We were dismissed but before we exited Whispering wind spoke. He would visit the chest in the morning and wanted me there. Mid morning was agreed upon as we made final eye contact and I heard the words;

"I look forward to your presence."

      No one of course was the wiser of our intimacy. I in turn nodded my head and turned to the robe covered doorway followed by Dan.

      The night air was refreshing and mind cleansing. I felt I was on a high. Dan and I walked slowly back to my car, said our goodnights and I set a course for home.

Chapter 19

It was nearing eleven o'clock when I parked at the motel. The night was perfect, I was still on a high. I grabbed a beer from the fridge and returned outside and relaxed in a deck chair admiring the star filled sky. Naturally my thoughts reverted to the chest. What special secrets does it hold and how do we open it ? I knew it belonged to the "Dineh" but I would even be against them forcing it open. It was a piece of ancient art unto itself.

I then drifted to Whispering Wind. This man genuinely intrigued me. I felt him to be a little like the king. A man of much knowledge. Not school book stuff but the wisdom handed down through the ages. The wisdom of nature itself.

I was anxious to see his reaction to the chest. It was apparent, from the reaction of others, this held special meaning for the people, for all people, not just the Navajo.

My eyes followed a shooting star which in turn led me to the constellation Orion. I laughed at myself. I wondered how many others had an imagination as active as mine. With that, I turned in. I knew I needed the rest.

Before crawling into bed I remembered the medicine I was given. I rubbed the salve into my leg and hip as thoroughly as I could. I poured the mixed powder into a glass of water. As it was mixing an odor arose that would have turned a skunk away. I was not going to question such ancient wisdom of healing herbs and I swallowed the potion as fast as I could. I had never tasted anything so horrible in my life. Its taste was worse than its smell. I refilled the glass with plain water hoping to rinse away the awful lingering taste.

I awoke refreshed and relaxed without a trace of pain or discomfort. What ever the shaman gave us was like a miracle cure.

I later learned from Dan he had the same results with the medicine. We were both like new men.

I took the time to fix a full breakfast which I thoroughly

enjoyed. I briefly thought of the Yucatan expedition but that would have to be put aside for now. I cleaned up and was at the school by noon. After some minor chit chat about nothing we walked to the council room. We could not help but admire the chest once more. "The Book" was also now on display. It had been carefully cradled in the fine oriental silk material it was found with. Hesitating to touch it I heard a voice in my head.

"Do not be afraid. You may touch it, open it if you will. You have earned the right."

I felt more than the voice, I felt a presence. I turned to find Whispering Wind behind me.

Dan repeated;

"He wants to see the chest."

Moving to its location Dan and I stood aside to allow the elder full access. Whispering Wind stood silent, his face taking on a whole new expression. More like astonishment and surprise. He mumbled a blessing to all four sides of the box. Stopping at the front again a sigh of recognition swept across his face. His eyes literally twinkled and a faint smile cracked his lips. He remained frozen like that for some time, a contentment shadowed his whole being and tears showed in his eyes.

He turned to us.

"Come." he said in perfect English. He headed for the door as we followed obediently.

It was about a twenty minute walk to the outer edge of the compound. I was surprised how agile Whispering Wind was and how fast his gait for one so close to being one hundred. Dan and I kept pace but were winded when we finally reached our destination.

Here before us was an old fashioned hogan. This one was six sided and looked to be about twenty five feet in diameter. This was Whispering Winds permanent home and had been for half a century. We were ushered into a world of living history. Window flaps were pulled aside high lighting his personal history. There were many hides and robes of deer, elk, antelope and buffalo and also blankets adorning the six interior walls that acted like sound proofing. Samples of ancient warfare and hunting were displayed openly. Bows, shields, armor of hides, war axes, lances, and battle clubs.

He obviously still slept on the floor on a bed of buffalo robes. There were many wooden crates and chests spread around the hogan. It looked crowded, yet spacious and lived in. Neither Dan nor I uttered a word we were so taken by this view of the past.

Whispering Wind indicated we sit on some boxes near the opening flap while he went to an antique chest full of memorabilia. Reaching in almost to the bottom he smiled a half smile and held up a deerskin bag tied at the neck. He wore a knowing glint in his eyes. Closing the window flaps he spoke again in English; "We go" and exited the hogan.

As earlier his walking pace was astounding. Dan and I smiled at each other as we struggled to keep up. Huffing and puffing we reached the council house and were very happy to be there. Whispering Wind went right to the chest with a confidence only a true believer possessed. He bowed before it mumbling some phrases neither Dan nor I understood. Turning partially toward us he untied the leather strapping of the pouch. From it he pulled another rectangular shaped bag of white deerskin repeating his previous words. He reverently reached in with thumb and finger removing a gold and silver object. At one end were metal zig - zags and curves at a slight offset angle. I looked on in total disbelief. This was the key to the chest.

Whispering Wind spoke to Dan explaining this special tool had been passed down for eons awaiting the reappearance of the lost chest. Dan questioned as to how long ago exactly. Whispering Wind did not know, only that it was long before the Spanish came. When the mountains were twice as high as the present time. This description made it impossible to calculate a time frame. I instantly decided not to try.

Feeling special yet again Whispering Wind handed me the key and pointed to the lock. I looked at Dan who was smiling his broad smile.

"**G**o ahead." he urged. "He wants you to open it."

I accepted the key from the elder and with a shaking hand inserted the key into its special opening. There was no resistance what so ever as I turned it and heard a loud click. I removed the golden tool and returned it to Whispering Wind who received it with a smile and a nod.

When the key was withdrawn the hasp quietly swung open. I took a step back to allow Whispering Wind the room to open the lid. He again urged me on to complete the unveiling of the contents. I almost did not want to open something so sacred but decided not to let my emotions rule me.

Gently holding the hasp I used my other hand to lift the lid. I guided it all the way back to a position one hundred and eighty degrees from closed. The heavy metal hinges held it securely.

The three of us stared at neatly stacked cloth bags and orderly scrolls and papers. Dan and I retreated slightly to give Whispering Wind first choice. He stood there contemplating his long lost history. Who knows what thoughts were going through his mind. Slowly he moved his arm to the chest gently touching the top most parchment. As he turned it over I caught a glimpse of markings neatly arranged on the face. Whispering Wind ever so gently ran his finger tips over the markings as a welcoming smile grew on his lips. He nodded his head up and down as if in approval or acceptance of their return. He passed the parchment to me and reached for another. This also had markings but were totally different. I now held the two for comparison. They were nothing alike nor had I seen either before. We viewed a scroll which was a third set of unidentified markings, nowhere close to the previous two.

With each paper or scroll touched Whispering Wind seemed to be more pleased. A sense of contentment appeared to fill his whole being. I felt his eyes upon me as my mind received a message.

"I am pleased, my young friend. Very pleased."

"The fact that you are pleased makes it all worth while Sir." I answered. That was the end of our dialog.

Lone Buffalo and I tried to keep the paper or parchments in order as best we could. I wanted to photograph everything before they were spread too far.

Half way through the papers Whispering Wind handed me one while he smiled and nodded his head in recognition. Turning it face up I also found it familiar. It was Chinese characters.

"How can that be." I thought. I immediately showed Dan who was as surprised as I was. He agreed we would talk to Whispering Wind later on.

Some documents bore similar markings while most were totally unlike any others. We carefully re-stacked the papers returning them to the chest for later study.

The bags or pouches were next. There was not much difference in size but the weight varied significantly. Our honored elder opened the first spreading the contents on a nearby table. A mixture of gold and silver flat pieces came into view. There were no markings on either side. Dan and I returned the pieces to the bag while Whispering Wind reached for another. This was coins of all sizes and shapes. Some showed designs on one side, some on both. These would definitely have to be studied in detail. Subsequent bags were gemstones, nuggets of gold, silver, copper and platinum. Another bag I recognized as early Egyptian or Sumerian coins. A few of these were even dated.

Work was really cut out for a study team for at least a few months I figured.

Each bag was unique in its manufacture and contents. A few bags even contained corn and a variety of other seeds.

~ ~ ~ ~

All was replaced and the chest closed and locked.

"**C**ome" instructed the elder and we obediently followed again. The room of our first meeting with the elders was our destination. Dove of Spring was already there. The two elders spoke quietly together. Eventually Dove of Spring joined Dan and I where we sat. Whispering Wind left noiselessly.

"**Y**ou may photograph all you want." said Dove of Spring seriously. "I'm sure you will do a thorough job. Of course we will want copies of everything."

"**T**hat goes without saying." I answered. "I hope to be able to put this in book form, chronologically if possible realizing that will take a lot of work."

"**O**ther details will be discussed tomorrow. Tonight you will join us again at the council fire."

She spoke as if it were a command no matter how polite it sounded. Then without another word she left.

Dan even looked confused as a result.

"**W**ell Pal, we at least get to have dinner together again." he smiled.

We had a light dinner at a local eatery, neither of us being too hungry, probably because of the excitement of what was to come tonight.

Dan did, however, mention another tribal member who was also an anthropologist slash archeologist. He was an older gentleman, a professor of anthropology at an eastern university. He did not recall the name.

"**I**'m sure he will be of great help when he returns for summer recess. His name is "Digger of Bones." laughed Dan.

"**A**ppropriate for the profession." I said.

"**S**teven Tallman is his white mans given name." Dan remembered "He has been studying the language of old for most of his life. Not just our own but European and Mediterranean also."

"**S**ounds perfect, perhaps I could get Mario to work together with him on the translation of the papers from the chest. Some of it appears to be Mayan, to my untrained eye anyway." I shot back.

"**M**aybe what we thought was going to be a problem won't be such a problem after all." Dan suggested.

"**O**ne can only hope." I replied.

"**W**ow look at the time. Dan said hurriedly. "We better get a move on. Dove of Spring does not take to kindly to tardiness."

I laughed softly as I spoke.

"**Y**ou're probably right, she did strike me as that type."

We quickly drove back to the school then made a bee line on foot for the council fire.

Others were still arriving as we neared the entrance.

"**L**ooks like we made it okay." remarked Dan.

We took our place as the last occasion as time moved quickly by and quietly waited. The history on the walls still drew my attention.

The drums started ever so quietly along with the chant. One could not help but feel the sacredness of this long followed tradition. Sky Above the Mountain appeared out of nowhere it seemed, and as before did a choreographed dance, three times around the fire throwing his magic dust into the flames for their dramatic flare up. Finished with his blessings he vanished as quickly as he arrived.

Dove of Spring chanted a few words then Whispering Wind arose looking directly at me.

*"**Y**ou will like what I am about to say. "* he murmured to my mind.

All I could do was nod in acceptance of his message.

Perfect attention was given to this respected senior. Naturally he spoke in the Navajo tongue while Dan again quietly translated.

*"**M**y children, I hold here a delicate antelope skin. On it is a trading agreement with the people from where the sun rises and where the sun sets. This has been in my possession since I earned my eagle feather. It was given to me by my father, from his father, and from his father, and his father, long before the Ancient Ones settled these lands. This is from the time of different peoples*

who arrived from places unknown to us, bringing new things and knowledge in exchange for our wisdom and gifts from. the Great Spirit. Because of these words we are joined with our brethren we can not see and do not know. The Great Spirit has allowed us to share in all others and others in us."

Whispering Wind paused looking around to everyone. He held up the antelope hide for all to witness.

"Until now" he continued. "This was the only proof of the legend. The Great Spirit, through an outsider, has seen fit to provide us with the true answer to this lost mystery. The newly discovered chest of the Ancient Ones, made in a far away land, is now returned to us. It has been protected by many similar words from many long lost nations. We have traded with them all in the past and this is proof of where our greatness came from. We are part of many nations and they are part of us. It is now our sacred duty to protect our history and to show today's world how great was our past."

Whispering Wind slowly reseated himself as Dove of Spring stood and announced clearly;

"**L**one Buffalo and Eric Dexter will now stand before the council fire.

Dan and I gazed at each other totally confused yet did as instructed. Dove of Spring again took control.

"**L**one Buffalo, you have brought pride and honor upon yourself and your people. Eric Dexter, you have brought pride upon yourself and our people."

She paused here then added;

"**S**oon to be your people."

Nervous and embarrassed once again I turned to Dan who, as usual was just smiling.

Whispering Wind now approached us followed by a

younger man holding a blanket. The pair stopped in front of Lone Buffalo first. Speaking in his native tongue he presented Dan with an eagle feather. Dan was obviously pleased as evident by his beaming smile.

Whispering Wind stepped to me. Still in the Navajo voice he uttered words, took the blanket from the young assistant and draped it over my right shoulder. He then took a leather strap, tied it around my head and reverently placed a long white eagle feather in the band. As he did so he voiced lowly words I did not understand. A chant, some what like a cheer, arose from the people.

Whispering Wind smiled warmly as he placed his hand on my shoulder. My mind heard him say;

"We shall talk later."

Whispering Wind then returned to his place with the elders.

Dan proceeded to tell me what had just transpired. I was now an honorary member of their nation and had been given the name "Hunter of Stories."

I could feel a tear in my eye as Dan aggressively shook my hand.

Dove of Spring smiling said;

"You are now one of us. Carry your name with pride and continue to bring honor to our name."

The fire was dying as the crowd shook my hand as they departed. I still felt overwhelmed at this unexpected acclaim. The participants finally cleared and Dan and I walked to the night air. Whispering Wind followed us out directing his words to Lone Buffalo. He nodded to me and took his leave. Dan repeated his message in English.

"He wishes to meet with both of us tomorrow mid morning at his hogan."

The walk back to the school was exhilarating. I felt different yet I felt the same. Jokingly I asked Dan if I had to wear the eagle feather all the time.

"That might be difficult, especially at night sleeping." he quipped back. "On the serious side." he continued, "The elders would find it quite respectful if you wore it to special functions, you know celebrations and the council fire, that sort of thing. You have a right to be proud my friend. The status of that white eagle feather is not given easily, it has to be earned."

We parted upon reaching the school and I continued alone to the motel. The first thing I did upon entering the room was to view myself in the mirror. One part of me thought it looked silly, the other part of me was proud. Another memory I could treasure. Setting it aside I got ready for bed. I thought I was too excited to sleep but drifted off in a matter of seconds.

~ ~ ~ ~

I slept like a baby, what ever that means. Most babies I know of do not sleep through the night. Oh well, I'm glad I did. A quick breakfast and I was off to meet Lone Buffalo. It took a bit longer to walk to the home of Whispering Wind since we were not keeping pace with him and we arrived without being winded.

We were eagerly welcomed with a cup of coffee and a comfortable place to sit.. Whispering Wind seated himself across from us where, to his side was an old box. From it he took the antelope hide we had seen at the council fire. He repeated his explanation of the hide while Dan translated. He passed the document to us. I felt a tingle shoot through my being just from holding such an ancient piece. I believe Dan felt the same from the look on his face. On the face of the hide, in perfectly neat order, were symbols inter spaced with a script of sorts. It meant nothing to Dan or I but Whispering Wind was able to read it.

"Now" the elder spoke, "I want you to compare it with the others."

"The others ?" I questioned in my mind.

Unbeknownst to us Whispering Wind had removed the other documents from the chest for his personal study. He handed one to us.

"This is from China."

This was obvious even to me, I recognized the Chinese characters. The format was the same as the one we held. An additional symbol, an Anasazi symbol, showed on the bottom. On close inspection of the first one was a Chinese character. They were like signed contracts of the period. Dan and I kept looking from one to the other and at each other.

With a knowing smile our host handed us another with his comment of;

"From the rising sun."

Again the same format. Dan and I both looked and sure enough the Anasizi symbol at the bottom. We asked to see another one. The smile on Whispering Wind's face told us he was aware that we understood what he was attempting to tell us. All the documents had the same symbol in the same place. They were all trade contracts or agreements from all over the world. Between peoples, who according to today's history writers should not have known each other. Yet here it was in black and white. Contracts between peoples thousand of miles away. This should make the established academic community wake up and listen and perhaps learn something.

I only recognized the Chinese and Mayan papers, though I could not read them. The rest were totally undecipherable, however they all followed the same format. I couldn't wait for an official translation.

Dan then questioned the contents of the pouches. According to Whispering Wind they were probably up front payment for goods received. The actual trade items were not paid for with coin or gemstones or money, so to speak. Goods were traded for equal value of the products being traded. That value was agreed upon by the parties at the time of trade. This seemed to be an equitable solution that kept all parties happy.

Dan and I agreed we received a wonderful history lesson. Too bad today's bargaining wasn't that forthright, instead of one trying to get the better of the other.

There was obviously a tremendous amount of work still to be done. No matter how accurate and real these documents may be, it will be extremely difficult to convince many scientists of their originality and time in history.

Whispering Wind must have tuned into my thoughts because I heard him say,

"This is as it has always been. Do not give up your beliefs."

I looked up into his eyes to see a serious concern. While still holding eye contact I answered;

"**I** will not falter in my knowledge of the truth."

His eyes softened with satisfaction.

Lone Buffalo realizing there was nothing more we could do at this time proceeded to help Whispering Wind put away the documents and pouches.

The wise one decided to walk with us back to the council room where he would return the treasured pieces of the past to the chest and lock it for safe keeping.

Whispering Wind even volunteered to walk at a slower pace so that we younger ones would not tire so easily. He said this with a knowing smile. We were both grateful to him. When all was secure at the council room including locking the room Whispering Wind excused himself and went his own way. Dan and I returned to the classroom where he had a class that afternoon. I went back to the desert, camera in tow.

~ ~ ~ ~

I knew there probably would not be anything else to find but I had grown accustomed to the lure of the desert as I had the jungle. I went straight to the pyramid knowing I wanted a second and more detailed inspection of the museum room. My thoughts kept going back to the map. It was apparent it was old, but just how old I wanted to determine for myself, if I could.

The pyramid appeared so lonely and deserted with out a thing for miles around. Deserted perhaps yet maintaining a serenity that was quite mind soothing. I detected some slight movement out of the corner of my eye. Mr. Blue approached, stopping about six feet away.

"Hello there my friend, you have a beautiful home here in the desert."

He stayed still as if listening.

"Sorry I have not seen you for a few days but I had other things to attend to."

"Here I am again talking to a large spider. They're really going to put me away some day. Oh well, I'm enjoying myself."

"I'm going to have a second look at the museum below, care to join me."

While Mr. Blue started crawling to the entrance while I fired up the generator. I chose not to remove the tarp from the doorway, instead just slipped passed. Mr. Blue was already in the makeshift elevator waiting for the ride down.

"Thanks for the company." I chuckled.

Once at the bottom we both walked to the chosen room. Before going to the map I took time to re-examine all the other artifacts.

The clothing designs and colors were astounding and the workmanship unmatched even today. The draw of the map was strong and kept pulling me to the earthen jar. I could fight it no longer so I gave in and proceeded to the bench that covered the jar.

Finally finding the correct scroll I was all thumbs trying to open it. Successful on my third try I found a few stones to keep it open and flat. I looked more closely this time at the dotted and dashed lines. Knowing what I knew now about the current flows in both oceans these marks appeared to follow the same path. But this wasn't just the flow of sea currents, these marks were tracking a sailing route. In a few places on each line were drawings of tiny ships, ships with sails. Most tracking either started or ended with China.. I had read of Chinese expeditions of discovery but was never witness to a map of their routes. This looked like just such a thing. The accuracy of the maps I found astounding. Not the super detail of today's maps but detail enough to identify the countries, coasts, rivers and bays which were obviously necessary for landings and settlements. Perhaps Columbus acquired such a map before he discovered the land that was already occupied by millions of people.

The rest of the day passed by rather fast, which it always seemed to do when you don't want it to. I returned the map scroll to the earthen jar and headed up and out. Not seeing Mr. Blue I killed the generator. I sat for a while enjoying the desert air before going to the motel. Tomorrow I wound start photographing the goodies from the chest.

Chapter 20

I was at the council room with my equipment set up before nine awaiting Whispering Wind with the key. He showed up within a few minutes along with Lone Buffalo.

*"**I** wish you luck, Hunter of Stories."* he said mentally as he unlocked the chest.

He smiled at me with his eyes as he spoke to Dan then turned and left. Dan had the usual message to notify Whispering Wind when I was finished so he could relock the chest. He then apologized for not being with me today but he was behind in his other responsibilities and had to tend to them.

"No matter," I told him. I would be quite busy for the day. In a way I was looking forward to a day alone. Sometimes my work was almost easier without distractions.

Dove of Spring stopped by in late morning. She was most polite and actually just curious. She wished me good luck and was gone in less than ten minutes.

Mid-afternoon, just as I was packing up my gear, Dan appeared.

"Just in time I see." he said. "I'll send a runner to get Whispering Wind to lock up. By the way Digger of Bones arrived just after noon. I filled him in briefly as to what we found, rather what you found. He wanted to settle in before we get together officially.'

"Just as well," I answered. "I'll probably be busy myself all day tomorrow. Perhaps we can arrange something for the day after."

Dan agreed as we went our separate ways.

I really did not have anything special planned but just wanted a few days to myself to let my mind catch up with what has occurred these past weeks.

Once home I forced myself to relax with a beer and quiet

music on the radio. I decided another day alone at the pyramid for additional photography and personal research would further relax me. A simple but leisurely dinner and I was asleep early.

~ ~ ~ ~

Up early and anxious to be in the desert I started out just as the sun was peeking over the low eastern hills. The day was proving to be quiet which filled me with a certain satisfaction I did not often feel. I was actually happy.

Arriving at my destination in such a good mood I sat in the shade of my car for close to an hour enjoying the peacefulness. I don't know when he arrived but I suddenly felt the presence of Mr. Blue sharing the shade of my car.

"Good morning." was all I said then turned my attention back to the stillness of the sandstone monuments. My friend and I shared the quiet for another twenty minutes, neither of us moving. The shadow of an Eagle soaring overhead broke the magic of the moment for both of us. I figured it was about time to earn my keep.

"Are you joining me today?" I asked Mr. Blue.

I thought I detected a hesitation but then he turned and crawled away in the opposite direction. I guess I would have to go it alone today.

I photographically documented our excavation and the outside of the pyramid from many angles before entering the structure itself. I then proceeded to continue my recording of the complete interior, up, down and all around. This now left me free to spend the afternoon reviewing the stored artifacts in detail.

Before I knew it, it was go home time. I had kept myself busy but I was not the least bit tired. I can't remember when I enjoyed my alone time so much. I even gave myself a treat of a nice Italian dinner on the way home. I was feeling so good I even stayed up for a while to watch the stars. It was later going to bed that I noticed the blinking light on the telephone. Dan left a message to meet him and Steven Tallman tomorrow about eleven in the morning at the council room.

~ ~ ~ ~

-The Ancient Ones-

"Steven Tallman, Eric Dexter." introduced Dan. "Or perhaps I should say Digger of Bones meet Hunter of Stories." He quipped.

All three men were smiling as Steven and Eric shook hands.

I did not like Stevens hand shake. Measuring the man mentally the gesture was without feeling. I found it to be practiced courtesy meaning nothing.

Steven Tallman was not what Eric was expecting. He guessed him to be in his early to mid sixties and guessed him to be about five foot nine inches tall. His posture and body were somewhat neglected. Too much classroom and easy living.

"I suppose he is measuring me also." I thought. *"His eyes will not stay focused on anything too long. Listen to me."* I scolded. *"You just met the man and already you're tearing him apart."*

I mentally apologized to the man yet, "a do not trust" feeling lingered.

"I understand you have spent some time discovering things about our people." commented Steven.

"That's not what I started out doing. It was just pure chance I happened upon them." I replied.

"How do you know these are genuine finds ? Are you a trained archeologist ?"

"Here it comes." I thought. *"Established Academia."*

"No, I am not but have worked with many for a number of years." I answered firmly.

Dan looking a bit upset jumped to my defense.

"I was with him on these discoveries, and as far as being genuine Whispering Wind and Dove of Spring and the elders have all reviewed them. They are real."

"Whoa, slow down Dan." Steven said back peddling a little. "I'm not making accusations, I'm just establishing some facts.

I also interrupted calmly.

"It's okay my friend, I can handle any questions Professor Tallman may have." I said to Dan while looking at Steven.

Steve Tallman got my message loud and clear. The battle was on. We automatically moved away from each other as is often the case with new adversaries. We three maintained a civility with forced half smiles, all hoping for the discussion to continue.

" **I** understand, Professor, you specialize in language of old. I'm sure we can use your expertise in the translation of the documents we found. Perhaps you could collaborate with some Mayan friends of mine who are well versed in the antique language and Glyph's of the Ancients." I offered.

With a haughty professorial attitude Steve answered;

"**T**hat would depend, I guess, on how genuine these so called documents are. I don't usually work with amateurs."

Keeping as calm as possible I answered slowly holding eye contact.

"**T**hese gentlemen are anything but amateurs. Their credentials are of the highest caliper recognized world wide."

Turning to Dan I continued;

"**P**erhaps, Dan, you can arrange with Whispering Wind a viewing of these "Documents" for Mr. Tallman."

I purposely emphasized the word documents. Without looking any further at Steven Tallman I left stating I still had paperwork to complete for the Smithsonian Institute. This of course was a lie, but only I knew that. I'll have to ask Dan about Steven's reaction to that statement, because I did not want to turn around.

Naturally, being a little upset I needed an outlet for my frustration. I did not want to cause a scene just then for I had no idea of the relationship of Mr. Tallman and the elders and the people in general. I slowly meandered to the hogan of Whispering Wind so I could defuse.

Luck was with me, the old man was home. As I approached I received a mental message.

"You may come in Hunter of Stories."

As soon as I entered I was handed a cup of hot black coffee and was directed to a soft pillow on the floor. I seated myself and Whispering Wind joined me with his own coffee. He smiled as I received his next words.

*"**I** can read that you have met Digger of Bones. Do not let him get to you my son. By blood he is still one of us but that is the only connection. He is no longer filled with the Navajo love and spirit. I'm surprised he even returns to us at all. He is filled with the white mans ways and has forgotten our traditions."*

I looked at him and answered,

"**Y**our wisdom comforts me Whispering Wind and from now

on I will try and act accordingly."

Nodding and smiling he replied;

"Now it is your wisdom that will guide you my son. The good heart will always triumph. Go now and be true to yourself."

As I walked back to Dan's classroom I felt refreshed as if my burden had been lifted. Deep inside I knew I had nothing to defend. Sooner or later the truth will always win out even if it is beyond my life span.

About the halfway point back to the classroom a familiar voice disturbed my thoughts.

"Beware, my young friend. There is one among you who is only out for personal gain."

Just as quickly my thoughts were my own again. I smiled to myself thinking this time I did not need the kings warning.

When I reached the classroom, I, luckily found Lone Buffalo alone who started talking as soon as he saw me.

"Im sorry Eric, I had no idea that Steven would be so haughty. I truly am sorry."

"No need to be Dan. People are who they are." I calmly replied.

"I had no clue he would be that way." Dan added.

"Not to worry my friend, perhaps we can still work together. At least we can try."

Dan was about to make another comment when Professor Tallman entered the classroom.

"I was just speaking with Dove of Spring. She seems to think that what you found is on the level. Maybe we got off on the wrong foot. That being said I thought you two could show me this pyramid every one is talking about."

"I think that would be a great idea." I replied. "You then can see first hand this small piece of history."

"I'm not saying I'm giving my blessing to this find but for the sake of the elders, I will keep an open mind."

"Understood and accepted." I answered.

"Good, suppose we plan on day after tomorrow." Steven said smiling. "That will give me time to settle some university business."

"**S**ounds okay with me." I commented.

"**Y**ou'll have to count me out on that. I have a field trip scheduled with the kids." Dan said with a disappointed voice.

"**T**hat's too bad." remarked Tallman with a wry smile. "But that will give Hunter of Stories and I a chance to get off to a better start."

My alarm signal went off in my head again but I smiled at his words anyway. The professor put out his hand again, as a peace offering I guess, and I accepted his non sincere hand shake once more.

"**T**hat's settled then, see you day after tomorrow. Meet you here ?" He asked as he left.

"**H**ere is fine." I called after him.

"**M**aybe he changed his mind after he spoke to Dove of Spring." Dan said enthusiastically.

"**A** leopard doesn't change his spots." I mumbled in return.

"**H**uh" Dan uttered looking confused.

That's the way I left him.

I went back to the motel and worked on putting my notes in some sort of order. I gave myself the rest of the day off deciding tomorrow would be a good library day again.

~ ~ ~ ~

There were very few people in the library which suited me just fine. I chose a back table out of everybody's way and sought out all the books on ancient maps I could find. It was slim pickings at best. I had to remind myself this was not a big city library. Nevertheless I managed a few books.

I made myself comfortable and started my search. I longed to have a copy of the scroll map for comparison but that would have to wait. I figured I would rely on my memory which was asking a lot I joked to myself.

The oldest maps shown in the books at my disposal were the Piri Re'is maps from fifteen thirteen but most were from the early fifteen hundreds and late fourteen hundreds. These were no more accurate than the scroll map. In fact I even questioned some particular areas. I should not criticize at all considering the time period. They did after all aide early European explorers in finding unknown lands of their time. At least unknown to the European peoples of that time period.

As interesting as the map information was it did not come near the date of the scroll map. I would have to wait for further study on this newly found map, if it is even accepted. I sat there for a while daydreaming of the first meeting of peoples from different parts of the globe. Obviously this did happen with knowledge being passed back and forth. How else would you find duplicate symbols, words, structures, cultural and religious practices.

My stomach told me it was time to depart and dinner out was the perfect solution.

Once home I turned on the TV, opened a beer and sat back to veg out. That's when I noticed the blinking light on the phone. Annoyed to get up again I retrieved the missed call.

Mr. Dexter, this is Steven Tallman. As I mentioned previously about getting off on the wrong foot, well to make amends I 'll pick you up tomorrow for our trip out to the desert. Lone Buffalo told me where you are staying so that's no problem. Let's say about nine-ish. See you then.

Talk about surprises, I was a bit taken aback.

*"**P**erhaps he has changed."* I thought. *"Not likely."* I answered myself and went back to the TV and beer.

Chapter 21

At two minutes to nine I noticed a car with Massachusetts Plates pull into the parking slot next to my car. Not waiting, I exited my cozy rooms locking the door behind me.

Steven Tallman, trying to look humble, met me by the front of the car, his hand extended. I accepted the same lifeless handshake squeezing a touch harder on purpose. There was no physical reaction yet I did detect a twinge in his eyes.

"Good morning." I offered with a big smile hoping to convince him I was genuinely pleased to see him, which was far from true. He gestured for me to get in the car and we were on our way. The small talk was strained, each of us trying to sound sincere.

Finally arriving at the pyramid, Steven appeared to take on a personality change. Academic haughtiness showed it's ugly head once again which I was quite comfortable with.

"Quite an undertaking." he said as he waved his arm spanning the whole complex. "How long did it take you to build this."

Catching me by surprise with his comment I answered defensively.

"I did not build this, it was discovered accidently while researching ancient roadways."

"Come now Mr. Dexter, or may I use the name Eric. You don't have to pretend with me. I'm not one of the children back there on the reservation."

I hesitated a moment collecting my wits about me and remembering the words of both the king and Whispering Wind of *"Be true to yourself."* My confidence regained, I was now prepared to take on Tallman's challenge.

"You may want to make fun of this discovery Steven, but I believe if you look seriously at what is before you, you will realize the great error you are making. You are being terribly unfair to yourself."

"**Y**ou expect me to believe this crap. You may fool the poor uneducated Navajo people but now you are talking with a professional of the archeological community. Do you know how stupid and silly this sounds. A pyramid in the American southwest, really now. The next thing you will be telling me is that the romans discovered America first."

I calmly smiled answering;

"**Y**ou're right, that would be silly."

Steven's eyes sparkled a touch, knowing he may have won until I continued.

"**T**hat would be silly because it was the Sumarian's and Minoan's long before Rome even was.

Tallman was now beginning to lose control of himself.

"**Y**ou have got to be kidding me. Is this some more of you rhetoric you're feeding the elders. They even believe you."

Re-grasping control of his slowly rising temper, he smiled slyly asking,

"**O**kay, Eric, let's get serious with each other. What's your game. What do you gain from this hoax. There's got to be some financial reward. So let me in on it and I'll back you up all the way. That way we will have these poor ingrates exactly where we want them."

It was an extremely difficult struggle but I stayed as composed as possible.

"**B**efore I justify your sick mind with an answer at least look inside with me. It will prove out what I am saying."

I didn't wait for an answer, I walked inside the pyramid and stepped into the mine elevator. With that still half smile on his face Tallman slowly followed. Down we went. Not looking at him I went to the turquoise room. Steven followed slowly and as he entered the room his expression became that of total surprise. A low whistle emanated from him, his eyes moving rapidly to every corner and pile of gemstone.

I quietly related to him the story of the dead miners, both the Ancient Ones and particularly the two Mayans. I could tell he was believing me although he was struggling to do so. As long as I had him on the edge I mentioned

"**A**nd further more we then discovered this."

I walked to the false pile of turquoise uncovering the hidden steps.

"**F**ollow me." was all I said as I descended. We entered the museum room to see Steven's expression change yet again.

I just could not resist rubbing it in a little.

"This was built more that a thousand years ago, but not by me. I emphasized."

I then proceeded to show him where the book lay for who knows how many centuries. Looking him straight in the eye I asked,

"**S**o how long do you think it took me to build this."

I think I actually detected a slight blush. He was caught at his own game. Recovering as quickly as he could.

"**W**ell, if you recall the other day I was just trying to establish solid facts. Archeology does not operate on just hearsay or supposition."

"**I** am well aware of that. I may not have the credentials you have, nor am I ignorant of procedures. I have worked along side professionals for some time and I have learned more than the basics. And as far as my Mayan friends, who you were so quick to write off, they also teach at the university level. They are not amateurs."

Professor Tallman held up both hands in defeat.

"**O**kay, you win. I was just trying to protect my people."

"**T**hat's funny, a few minutes ago you were willing to do a fleece job on them."

Steven's face suddenly took on a evil look. He recovered quickly and smiled.

"**O**h I was just playing along to see how far you would go. No offense meant."

It was all I could do to restrain myself. I really wanted to leap at him and beat him silly. It took every bit of professionalism I had to even look at him again.

Steven spoke again as if nothing had happened. It was obvious he was playing to my good side when he stated,

"**I**t looks like you really hit the jackpot with this one. This should rewrite some history books."

Then he anxiously added,

"**I** understand you found a buried chest also. Was that near here ?"

My radar went off again. I did not know how to take this sudden interest of his.

Expecting but not expecting it was the Kings voice.

"You are wise to be alert, Eric. All on the surface is not real. Beware."

Before I could even think about answering the voice trailed away to nothing.

The kings voice and message was enough to fortify my resolve to see Tallman's game through.

"Not too far." I answered innocently.

We exited the pyramid and I notice he was holding a rather large chunk of turquoise. I said nothing.

After readjusting the tarp for security we returned to his car. Mr. Blue was waiting for Mr. Tallman. Sighting my blue friend he kicked sand in its direction. "Scat" he yelled. "I hate those disgusting creatures."

Pretending no interest I ignored the incident thinking the feeling is probably mutual. As far as I was concerned he did not rate an explanation of our relationship.

We made the short drive to the sandstone sentry. I was astonished by his reaction to the beauty of the wind sculpted mini mountain. I didn't think he had any appreciation for nature's beauty. I laughed internally.

As we neared the uncovered shaft Tallman made a comical comment, pretending interest, of course, about the backhoe. We carefully maneuvered ourselves to a safe position to allow us to view down the shaft. The Sun's angle was enough to provide some light though not quite enough for picking out any detail.

"What's that." inquired Steven. "That bright spot." he pointed. I tried to gage where he was pointing when I felt my legs being kicked out from under me and found myself hurtling down the partially open shaft. I hit bottom with a terrible thud. Barely conscious I felt small rock and gravel falling on me. Painfully trying to gaze upward I saw the wooden platform fall over the opening. All was now dark and as the external light disappeared, so did my internal consciousness.

~ ~ ~

I regained awareness of my surroundings with more pain than I had felt in years. I lay there as part of the dirt that covered me. Once I felt awake enough I tried moving, starting with my head. My neck hurt a bit but at least it wasn't broken. I knew I was going to have some headache. Methodically I inventoried my entire body with slow somewhat painful movements. Convincing myself that nothing was seriously broken, I moved to a sitting position. I felt around with my hands finding nothing. I tried standing but that was a no go. My left hip and upper thigh did not want to cooperate with the rest of me. The prone level was almost intolerable. Shifting my weight to my right leg I finally managed an upright position. As luck would have it the ladder was nearby which allowed for much additional support. Knowing where the ladder was helped my orientation in the dark. I was grateful to have that added measure of assurance that I did not fall victim to the sunken hole that once housed the chest. I gave myself the necessary time for my body to adopt to my limited movement situation.

I thought of climbing the ladder which would be a great risk in the dark knowing I would not be able to push open the heavy wooden platform sealing my temporary grave.

Using the wall as a guide I moved away from the ladder remembering there was ample room behind the hole. I felt the floor there would not have as much dirt and rubble. It would grant me a much wanted smoother surface to sit or lay on. The slow movement of my good foot kicked something which echoed a familiar sound. Taking my time I managed to find the object in question. I was right. It was the lantern I dropped when I was crushed by the chest against the ladder. Keeping my fingers crossed I found the switch. "Click." and there was light.

It's amazing how much better one feels to see where you are moving. I could not move any faster but there was an added confidence. Attaining my goal I sat down to rest my hurting body. No matter what it takes, stay calm, I counciled myself. I rested by one of the wooden paneled walls trying to find a comfortable position for my left leg. To keep my mind working I scanned the area with the lantern. Lo and behold there was Mr. Blue.

"You are a sight for sore eyes, Pal. Now if you could only carry me out of here." I said knowing that was not possible. Without hesitating Mr. Blue turned and crawled to the wall to my left. He disappeared under the bottom board. About five or so seconds later he reappeared coming a little closer to me. He stopped momentarily then repeated the motion disappearing under the wall.

A slightly longer span of seconds and he emerged moving even closer to me. Mr. Blue undertook the same action for a third time remaining out of sight for a longer period. As if by magic he materialized out from under the wall board this time stopping only a foot or so away from me.

"You want me to follow you. Is that it old friend ?" If only I was that small."

Pushing my doubts aside and as hurtful as it was, I moved closer to the wall in question. I loosened some dirt where Mr. Blue had crawled under. Once I had my fingers under the wall I felt nothing on the other side. Just space. I pulled my hand back and used it to knock on the boards. I received a knocking echo. Hollow came to mind.

"How can that be." I voiced out loud.

I rapped the wall again, the same hollow sound was returned. Quickly finding my pocket knife I began scratching and chipping away. It took time but I finally did manage a hole. More strenuous chiseling and I had a hole big enough to look through with the lantern. It was an open space that went on forever.

After a short break I used my good leg, good being a relative term. It hurt the least, to kick at the boards. It took some effort but I at last gained an opening large enough to crawl through. Mr. Blue preceeded me.

I found us in a tunnel. Narrow though it was, one could maneuver in a crawl. My light showed it going up at a slight incline. I could not see an end. Hopefully this went up and out. Before continuing, I decided to rest a while to reestablish some stamina. Mr. Blue sat with me.

"Thanks Pal, I can use the company. Right now I don't care what people may say about talking to a large spider. You are my confidence and my hope."

Feeling somewhat renewed, discounting the pain, I moved to my belly and started to crawl. My left leg was not much help, so between my two arms and one leg I was making progress, slow though it was. Mr. Blue stayed with me keeping about five feet ahead. I was pushing thirty minutes and had to stop. I rolled over on my back and rested. Mr. Blue remained with me.

I judged my distance traveled to be about one hundred feet. Thinking back to when I walked the perimeter I had judged it to be about four hundred yards. So if this tunnel was running parallel with the length, and subtracting about a third because of where this shaft is located leaves about eight hundred plus or minus feet. After what I traveled so far should leave about seven hundred feet. At the rate I'm able to crawl I'm looking at another three or four hours. Let's hope they didn't build this tunnel completely to the other end.

Why this tunnel anyway ? Then it dawned on me the great

pyramids of Egypt all had secondary hidden entrances. Could it be this was modeled after that style. Judging by the newly found scrolls there was trade and communication with the Middle East and the Mediterranean over a thousand years ago.

Enough philosophical brain drain. I scolded myself. Back to crawling.

As soon as I turned over Mr. Blue took off without getting too far ahead of me. Crawl, rest, crawl, rest It seemed like a lifetime before I hit a dead end. Instant despair set in when I hit the solid wall of rock. I truly needed a rest now and my blue friend was no where to be seen. The lantern was also becoming dim . I switched it off, rolled on to my back and passed out.

~ ~ ~ ~ ~ ~

Lone Buffalo, having just returned from his field trip, was cleaning out the bus when he noticed Professor Tallman approaching.

"Well, how did you like your visit to our desert pyramid ?" he asked all smiles.

"I wouldn't know." Steven replied in all innocense. "Eric never showed up. Perhaps he had something else to do and just forgot Another time maybe."

"That's not at all like him., I'll call him at the motel later. First I have to put the finishing touches on this field lesson." commented Dan.

"No need to push. I'll be leaving tomorrow   morning anyway." Returned Tallman. I can view your pyramid another time."

"That's fine with me Professor, I'll see you on your next visit. Good luck."

Thanks, and give my regards to Eric." said Steven as he walked away smiling.

Dan returned his attention to the bus.

Later that evening Dan tried Eric's motel room number several times with no answer. "He must be out for the evening." he thought. "No sense in leaving a message." I know I'll see him tomorrow."

~ ~ ~ ~ ~ ~

It took a while to realize where I was and why it was so dark. Finally collecting my wits I reached for the lantern. Lighting up my surrounds made me feel better. Actually the sleep made me feel much better. The aches and pains were still there but I was able to move a little easier. The return of Mr. Blue did a lot to perk up my spirits. He also, looking as if he was happy to see me, scooted right up the wall I was facing. At about the halfway point he reversed directions.. When he reached bottom he began to dig. I moved to where he was, took out my trusty pocket knife and joined in the digging.

It wasn't too long before we hit wood. It was now time for some foot action again. Only a few kicks and the wall gave way. There was the sudden rush of fresh air. I drank in as much as I could as fast as I could. It had not dawned on me just how stale the air was. My head started to feel clearer.

My lantern showed we had broken through to the outside. I carefully made my way over the rubble to see the star lit sky. Talk about the renewal of ones spirit.

Sitting right beside me was my furry blue friend.

"I thank you my friend. I owe you big time for this rescue and I won't forget it. You saved my life."

He didn't even twitch but somehow I knew he heard me.

I had to make a plan now that my small panic was subsiding. Allowing my common sense to return I decided against traveling the desert in the dark. There were just too many obstacles and I was hurting too much already. I knew where I was now and have some shelter. I could also use more rest. That's it then, I sleep now and wait for daylight.

It took a while but I finally made a comfortable spot just inside the opening. I lay down as best I could and studied the stars. There again was Orion. I often wondered what the exact draw was for this particular constellation, especially for people so widely separated from each other. The layout of the pyramids of Egypt followed this star cluster. The ancient ones of the desert had laid out their major centers according to the Orion design. Why ? What is the significance ? I'm sure if I was to do an in depth research of the long ago civilizations I would find the same use of Orion.

My relaxing study of the starry heavens performed its task perfectly fore the next thing I awoke to was the sun in my eyes.

~ ~ ~ ~

I was now facing a twelve to fifteen mile walk back to the reservation complex. My left hip and knee were pretty well bruised but I don't think broken. No matter it was still difficult to walk. I didn't have much of a choice so I started my long hobble.

After just a few yards ; "Wait a minute." I said out loud. "The backhoe. Not the best vehicle for a ride but at least it beats my imitation of walking. I looked down the side of what was my stone prison and spotted the yellow machine. It would be worth the twenty minutes walk back in the opposite direction.

I struggled up into the cab. No key. I searched as best I could but no key. A few minutes of feeling sorry for myself brought me to a decision. Try jump starting the engin. I used to do it with cars, it can't be that different. My pocket knife to the rescue again. It was a struggle hanging upside down but I was able to make contact. The "Rrrrr, Rrrrrr, Rrrrrr" sounded wonderful but that's where it ended. No matter how many times I tried, The engin would not kick over. I gave up when the battery grew weaker.

Frustrated again I rested. Climbing out of the cab I checked the gas tank. Dry as a bone.

I looked in the direction I had to go and saw nothing but desert haze forever. Finding some broken boards I fashioned a makeshift crutch. Far from the greatest invention in the world but it worked. It made my hobble a bit more tolerable.

A struggling hours walk brought me to more desert.

"**F**unny, when you're driving, it doesn't seem this desolate." I mused. "Time to sit for a while."

Never mind sitting, I lay down. The hip almost stopped hurting when I did so. Not wanting to but I apparently fell asleep. The noise and shadow of a vulture scared me back to life.

"**Y**ou've got a long way to go before I become your dinner pal. I was up and moving again.

It was noon as I pushed myself towards my second hour. At least the vulture gave up. A small sand stone growth provided shade and a back rest for my next stop. A light desert breeze was most welcome. My body demanded more time but after a half hour I forced myself up and plodded on with my crutch. I pushed myself well beyond an hour before I was forced from exhaustion and pain to stop again. I tried not to think of the water I so desperately needed.

Catching up with the good Professor was my goal that kept me going. On my feet I moved to the never nearing horizon.

~ ~ ~ ~

I didn't understand why but things were becoming blurry and this was happening more and more frequently. I guessed a circus must have come to town because I was seeing horses and elephants. Even a giraffe now and then. I must be part of the show. I thought, particularly with me being surrounded by all these beautiful animals. There's the ring master and he's calling my name. Here I am sir, over here. I shouted as I waved my arm.

"Whoa, calm down Eric, you'll rip out the I V"

I felt a pressure on my arm pushing on something soft and cool.

"It's okay Eric, you're safe now. You're going to be okay. Lay back and rest."

I recognized the voice of Lone Buffalo and opened my eyes to his forever smile.

It took a few minutes to realize I was in a hospital bed with my left leg immobilized. I looked at Dan and he read the question in my mind.

"I found you in the desert, passed out. Well, you were actually going out of your mind. I don't understand why you were walking, but I couldn't find your car either."

Slowly it all came back to me.

"How long have I been here /" I inquired.

"Since late afternoon the day before yesterday." Dan answered.

My head, becoming clearer by the second, I questioned.

"Tallman, is he still around ?"

"He left two days ago, Why?"

"Did he know I was here ?"

"No. I brought you here just after he left. He said to give you his regards when I saw you."

"That SOB I mumbled." Then looked at Dan's curious expression as he asked.

"He said you never showed for your trip to the pyramid. Where were you?"

I settled back and caught my breath and told the story of that day's events including my night in hell.

"**H**ow did you find that secondary escape tunnel ?"

I smiled at Dan but before I could answer he did for me.

"**D**on't tell me it was Mr. Blue." he laughed.

"**O**kay, I won't." I laughed with him.

A thought passed through my mind. I interrupted our laugh.

"**H**as anyone checked the scrolls or documents from the chest ?" I asked hurriedly.

"**Y**ou can't be serious ?" Dan questioned in return.

"**D**ead serious." I remarked. "Get back to the council room and hurry.   I'm very serious Dan. I mean it. Get in touch with Dove of Spring and Whispering Wind right away also. While you're doing that I'll work on getting out of here."

"**Y**ou can't do that Eric. You have been through a lot, you need to rest. I can handle it. Please lie back, I'll do as you ask and get back here ASAP."

Dan left the infirmary almost running. I found a pad and pencil in the drawer of the bed table and proceeded to write down the license plate number of the professors car as bold and clear as possible. I also added the year make and model along with the color. I figured the police would want these later. I lay back trying not to think of my discomfort.

I must have dozed off because the next thing I was aware of was a presence in the room. I opened my eyes slowly and saw Dan, without his smile along with Dove of Spring. Dan obviously waited until he thought I was fully awake.

"**Y**ou were right, I'm sorry to say. The documents from the chest are missing and Whispering Wind does not have them, nor does he have the key."

"**A**nd the scrolls ?"

"**I** still have a few that I am studying, the rest are also missing." admitted Dove of Spring.

"**T**he map scroll ?" I asked hesitantly.

"**A**mong the missing." she answered sheepishly.

I could feel myself physically starting to tremble. First from the precious history now missing and combined with anger that I usually don't let get this far in me.

In a gesture I did not expect, Dove of Spring put her hand on mine that was both warming and comforting.

"We will get them back, I promise you." She underlined her words with a genuine loving squeeze of my hand.

This unexpected motion had a calming and defusing effect on my shaking. I took a deep breath and thanked her. It was the first time I was aware of her warm smile. I turned again to Lone Buffalo;

"Has Whispering Wind been made aware of this ?"

"Yes, but first and foremost he was concerned for your health. Both he and Sky Above the Mountain went to the sacred place to offer prayers for your recovery. He will come to see you after that."

Except for my parents, never in my life can I remember people being this caring for me. It gave me a lot of food for thought which I ran through my mind.

"We have already notified our reservation police. They in turn will make contact with the proper authorities with the county and state."

I indicated the paper on the bedside table. Dan picked it up and had his smile back.

"Always thinking ahead I see. I'm sure this will be of great assistance. I will get word of this out right away."

Dan turned to the door just as Whispering Wind and the medicine man were entering.

Dove of Spring spoke quietly with another squeeze of my hand.

"I will take my leave now."

Whispering Wind waited till both were gone before speaking with his mind.

"Our chameleon has finally shown his color. Not to worry my young friend. All will be recovered."

To me these were more than just words. It was a guarantee which had a healing effect on my disturbed mental anguish. Whispering Wind knew this. He then added,

"Sky Above the Mountain has prepared a special potion for you. Please do not fight it."

A dark powder was mixed in the water glass.

"Drink quickly." directed the holy man.

I did as instructed trying not to react too strongly to the

vile taste and smell. Both men were nodding and smiling at me.

"You will rest now my son."

I felt his words as a cloud of euphoria overcame me and my visitors seemed to vanish..

~ ~ ~ ~

A lovely young and very sweet nurse informed me upon awakening that I had just slept eighteen hours. I felt like a million bucks. My left hip and thigh were now only a slight discomfort.

"Now don't get too confident Mr. Dexter. You don't want to undo all that has helped you.

"Is that awful stuff I took on the commercial market ?" I inquired.

"No Sir. And it probably never will be. The Federal Drug Administration doesn't take to kindly to old fashioned natural medicine. We keep these things to ourselves. We know what works and what doesn't. You may walk up and down the corridor twice but then I want you back in bed."

"Yes Mam. You're the boss." I happily answered. I knew she was right and I didn't want to upset her, or Whispering Wind for that matter.

Dan visited me just after noon carrying my lunch tray. It was all normal food I was delighted to see. He brought me up to date on the progress of locating the esteemed professor. It appeared to be a foregone conclusion that he would be apprehended, and most likely very soon.

~ ~ ~

Lone Buffalo then proceeded to tell me of a new project he and the students were undertaking. They were going to excavate more of the pyramid and construct a more secure entranceway. They wanted to preserve it as a museum as part of their heritage.

I expressed my support for such a project and wished them success. That is when Dan dropped the surprise on me. The museum was to be called "The Eric Dexter Navajo Heritage Museum" He said this of course accompanied by his gigantic contagious smile.

I felt a blush come over me and before I could comment, Dan held up his hand to stop me.

"This was totally the youngsters idea. I had nothing to do

with this. They want to honor you for what you have given them, another piece of their heritage. They even received the approval of the elders before I was informed."

"None of this is necessary. I don't rate this kind of honor" I said humbly.

"You may think that Hunter of Stories, but don't break up a dream of the young ones. This is for them also. A story for their grandchildren."

Still flushed with embarrassment I accepted Dan's reasoning.

Changing the subject Dan asked if I enjoyed my nice long nap.

"The nap was fine." I answered. "What I had to do to get there was horrible." I joked.

"You're right, that stuff is pretty bad." We laughed.

~ ~ ~

Dove of Spring appeared again. I felt honored with her concern.

"I'm glad you're here Dan. The news I have is for both of you. I was contacted by the state police. They were informed by the state police of Louisiana that they have located the vehicle matching the description we supplied.."

Dan and I smiled at this news. I started to reply but was stopped.

"There's more. A man matching the professors profile was seen entering a building they have had under surveillance."

Questioning looks appeared on our faces as Dove of Spring continued.

"Under surveillance along with the FBI. Apparently there is an international group dealing in illegally appropriated rare documents. They are sold to the highest bidder of unknown collectors. Mostly collectors of rare historical papers and maps. Then they are never seen again. To the best of their knowledge our papers have not changed hands yet. They do however expect some sort of transaction soon. The FBI has identified some foreign high bidders in and around New Orleans."

"You really know how to tell a story to keep listeners in

suspense." remarked Dan.

Dove of Spring smiled while continuing,

"**T**here question is now, can we identify said documents and make a positive ID of Tallman. The professors ID is no problem but what of the documents."

Lone Buffalo grinned as usual.

"**Y**ou tell her Eric, it's your show."

Looking directly at her I replied,

"**I** have everything photographically documented from the instant of discovery to it's housing in the council room.."

Now Dove of Spring was smiling as well.

"**I** even have one better than that. Wait till he sees me, now that I'm not dead."

She was outwardly happy with my statement.

"**T**his will work well. I wish you a speedy recovery Eric."

"**A**fter this news I feel recovered already."

She flashed the biggest smile I've seen to date.

"**I** like your respect of my Navajo name. I am also known as Violet. My mother loved the spring flowers."

"**T**hank you." I smiled as she turned and left the room.

Dan and his silly grin chided,

"**N**ow you are really on the in. I think she likes you."

I shouldn't have but I felt chagrined and humbled yet again. I didn't mind Dan's kidding, I knew he meant nothing by it. I would probably do the same to him if given the opportunity.

Now it was just a waiting game. I actually did feel much improved, what with the recent news received and some real nourishment. I soon found myself alone again, everyone having departed to continue their busy day.

I sat on the edge of the bed staring out the window at nothing in particular. I reflected on the past few days and thought about how lucky I was to have the friends that I have. I sometimes wished everyone could have a life as fulfilled as mine. There I go getting mushy again. I've got to learn to grow up.

"There is nothing wrong with your view of life

-The Ancient Ones-

Eric. That is why you could be a chosen one."

I expected the king to show sooner or later. This was perfect timing.

"**C**an you help us recover these valued documents Atol ?" I inquired. "I think we could use your help. Not for me, but for these people."

*"**Y**ou underestimate yourself my friend. You need not my help. You already have everything under control. Justice will prevail as long as you wish it so. Again you have made me proud. Heed the council of Whispering Wind and your wishes will be fulfilled.*"

As I pondered the king's words I realized I was alone. I continued looking outside at nothing until a soft voice from behind brought me back to the present.

"**M**r. Dexter, it is Sky Above the Mountain's wish that you rest again. It is for your own good." the sweet voice added.

I turned to her, not to argue but to ask;

"**W**hat is your name besides Florence Nightingale."

She gave me a big grin answering,

"**I** am called Little Faun. That is the only name I was given."

"**A**nd a very appropriate one." I complimented.

She blushed and I could see I made her uncomfortable. To let her recover I asked about the medicine man, whether or not he had a given name that was not Navajo.

"**I**f he does I do not think anyone knows. He is always just the holy man or medicine man known as Sky Above the Mountain." she answered politely.

"**N**ow please, it is time for you to rest."

"**O**kay, I'll agree to that on one condition."

She looked at me questioningly.

"**P**lease call me Eric."

She smiled and said "Thank You."

There was a trace of a blush again as she turned and left the room. I made myself comfortable and closed my eyes and pretended I could hear my jungle serenade.

~ ~

A quiet restful night had me feeling absolutely wonderful the next day. Little Faun brought me a full breakfast which I devoured. Before I could ask she smiled and answered,

"**I** am told, Eric." she said my name feeling shy, "That you may leave here today. Please Sir don't get too physically carried away. Give yourself a few more days to completely heal."

"**I**'ll do whatever you say, Little Faun and I thank you for putting up with me."

She half smiled as she left the room.

Dan popped in with some clothes that did not quite fit, since mine were pretty much destroyed from my latest ordeal.

"**T**hese will at least get you out of here then I can drive you to your motel to get some clothes that fit. On the drive there Dan said that Dove of Spring wanted to meet with us just after lunch. Apparently there is a breakthrough of the search for Tallman. That's all I know."

"**W**ell I guess we'll just have to wait then. Thanks for the ride but I think I'll take my own car back. I'll meet you at your office in a few."

Lone Buffalo and I had a light lunch prior to our meeting with Dove of Spring. We speculated about the information she might have then decided we were just building ourselves up for a possible letdown. To change the subject Dan asked about my prison shaft. What should we do with it ?

"**I** have given that some thought." I suggested. "I think we should make another thorough search and if we find nothing then close and seal it. Of course with the approval of the elders."

"**A**re you sure you want to go down there again ?"

"**S**ure, why not. I don't usually let my graves bother me too much" I joked.

"**O**kay Pal, if it doesn't bother you that sounds like a plan. Do you really think we will find anything else ?"

"**N**o I don't but if you remember the pyramid, it was one thing after another. So let's make sure before we close it up. I just remembered, the backhoe is out of gas."

"**I** can take care of that." Dan commented.

"**L**ook at the time. Where are we supposed to meet Dove of Spring ?"

"**M**y office " Dan answered as we stood to leave the cafeteria.

Dove of Spring was waiting for us. Dan apologized for us while Violet and I smiled at each other.

"**I**'m pleased to see you looking well, Eric."

"**T**hank you , Violet, I do feel so much better thanks to Sky Above the Mountain."

Dan now wearing his silly grin interrupted.

"**D**on't keep us in suspense any longer, what's the big news you have."

Violet turned serious stating;

"**T**hey have apprehended Professor Tallman with goods in hand."

"**W**ho did?." Dan asked anxiously.

"**T**he FBI in cooperation with the Louisiana State Police and the local Sheriffs Department. Not only did they get Tallman, but apparently rounded up big time dealers in the selling of historical documents. They have been working on this scam for many months. The FBI is quite pleased with this roundup of both buyers and sellers and it will be up to us, or rather you Eric, to put the finishing touch to this investigation. Of course the good professor is claiming his innocence. The FBI is bringing Tallman here, along with our documents, for identification."

"**T**hat's great news." I commented with open satisfaction.

"**W**e can get back to work on the translation and interpretation of the contracts and the maps." added Dan.

"**T**hey should be here this time tomorrow."

Violet continued with concern. "Are you sure you're up to this Eric ? We can put this off if need be. Your health is more important."

"**I**'m more than fine Violet." I smiled at her. "In fact I cant wait for this. Let's call it payback.

"**I** can't wait to see this also." Dan chided in. "You two will have to excuse me, I have some class work to catch up on." he said as he politely rushed Violet and I out of his office.

Although he tried to hide it, I detected a sly grin.

I found myself outside and alone with Violet. It was an awkward moment for both of us. I broke the silence.

"**I** want to visit Whispering Wind and thank him for his help and faith in me."

"**W**ould you mind if I walked with you ?" she asked quietly.

I couldn't answer fast enough.

"**I** would like that very much. We can talk more about tomorrow and the FBI."

Looking rather disappointed Dove of Spring answered coldly,

"**I**f that's what you wish."

"You dummy, that was a hell of a thing to say." I scolded myself. To make amends I spoke more from my inner self.

"**N**ot really" I said, "I just did not know what else to say."

Violet brightened up with a broad warm smile.

"**H**ow about just being yourself." she replied. "Tell me more about this king of yours. He sounds intriguing."

"**T**hat he is, or was, or still is. I get myself confused sometimes."

Violet chuckled quietly at that but urged me to go on.

I gave her a quick synopses of my two seasons in the Yucatan, to which she was very attentive. Before I realized it we were at the hogan of Whispering Wind. As we approached he opened the covering flap of his home. Dove of Spring looked surprised by this. I could see the question in her eyes.

"**Y**es, we communicate the same way." I answered.

Again she flashed her warm smile.

We accepted the cool lemonade he offered.

Whispering Wind chose to live without the convenience of electricity. The drink was cooled by the old fashioned evaporation method. The elder statesman was pleased to see both of us and spoke at length with Violet in their native tongue of course. He would interrupt now and then to communicate with me. To date everything had his approval.

Our lemonade finished and the conference over, just like the king you knew when you were excused. As we were leaving I received another message.

"You will do well Hunter of Stories. We will seek each other when all is done."

I could feel Violets eyes upon me. I gazed at her shy smile.

"You were conversing again." she remarked.

I returned her smile and shook my head yes.

"I wish I could do that." she added

"You can." I answered her. "It is all a matter of how open your mind is."

"Can you teach me ?"

"I can try, but not now. My mind is too busy preparing for tomorrow."

Dove of Spring accepted this. I could also read her thoughts about spending more time with me. I smiled internally not knowing what to do with this growing situation. We walked slowly and silently back to the school and found Dan in his office..

"I'm glad you're back Eric. The young ones wish to share some things with you."

I turned to Violet saying,

"Do you mind ?"

Looking disappointed and almost hurt, she answered.

"No, you go ahead, I have something else to do. We'll catch up another time."

Without saying anything else she turned and left. Dan caught on to the look she had.

"Did I interfere with something ?" he inquired.
I half smiled mumbling.

"No it was nothing."

Chapter   22

I awoke early, showered and had a full breakfast. I was on my second cup of coffee when the phone rang. Expecting to hear Dan's voice I was surprised to hear the soft voice of Violet. Without thinking I said;

"**I**t's good to hear your voice."

"**I**s it. She replied. "I'm glad."

I kind of knew that would be her response, but leading her on was the last thing I wanted to do. *'I'll have to work on that later."* I thought.

"**A**ny news from the FBI ?" I asked immediately.

"**Y**es, as a matter of fact that's why I'm calling. They expect to arrive about one thirty this afternoon."

"**G**ood, I'll plan on being there by eleven thirty. That should give me time to settle in and get my car hidden away." I said in a professional tone.

"**W**e are going to meet at the conference room, the elders will be present." With her answer she took the same cool professional tone as I.

I hoped we could sort this out at a later date when we were both free of present worries.

"**W**ill Whispering Wind be there ?" I inquired politely.

"**M**ost definitely. He wants to address other concerns."

"**S**ounds interesting, Do you know about what?"

"**N**ot really, Whispering Wind can be a very private person when he wants to. We will have to wait and see." Violet replied in a softer voice."

*"**P**erhaps she's not to angry."* I thought.

Also softening my voice "I'll see you later."

"**Y**es, later " she echoed and hung up.

"**Y**ou will talk to that nice lady later on, won't you?" I chastised myself.

-The Ancient Ones-

~ ~ ~ ~ ~ ~

Arriving at the time promised I hid my car away from the normal travel lanes and walked to Dan's classroom. Dove of Spring was already there and we exchanged warm smiles. Violet was the one who would be heading up the meeting although questions from all the elders were expected. We reviewed our plan with me being out of sight until the appropriate moment. In case the FBI was to arrive early we three left for the conference room. There I tucked myself away in the small anti-room supplied with my additional photo evidence and a large lemonade.

"Don't run away." joked Violet as she closed the door to a crease so I could hear the proceedings. Luckily there were a few wildlife magazines in the room to keep me occupied while I waited.

It was a touch after one PM when, one by one the elders entered the meeting room going to a pre assigned seat. The table seating had been arranged so that Professor Tallman would be seated with his back to the anti-room. Whispering Wind was the last to enter along with Dove of Spring.

At one thirty two Dan arrived with our escorted guest of honor, who was shown his special seat. There were three FBI agents. One stood aside while the other two were seated on either side of the professor. Brief introductions were made, annoying the esteemed Mr. Tallman.

"Okay, okay, can we get on with this charade ? I have better things to do with my time. Who is in charge and what is this all about ?" said the Professor in a full of himself huff. He was answered in the calm authoritative voice of Dove of Spring.

"In good time, Digger of Bones, in good time." Turning her attention to the standing agent; "Now, Mr. Spencer, so that we are all clear on our stories, you apprehended Mr. Steven Tallman at our behest. Is that right ?"

"That's correct." he replied.

"And in his possession were certain ancient artifacts that belong to the Navajo nation.

"I still don't know what this is all about." protested Tallman. "What was in my possession was my personal property." he added in a raised voice. The agent to his left slowly put his arm over to gently touch Steven who in turn gave him a very mean, annoyed stare.

Ignoring the professors interruption, Dove of Spring continued.

"It is also my understanding Mr. Spencer that you determined that Professor Tallman seated in front of you was there to sell the afore mentioned objects."

"Yes Mam, that is our contention."

"And what led you to that conclusion if I might ask."

Well Mam," replied Agent Spencer, "We have been monitoring the location in question for quite sometime. Mr. Tallman here," he indicated the professor, "and others by the way, were there with the full intent of selling the artifacts in their possession. For your further additional information this is not the first time Mr. Tallman has appeared on our surveillance cameras."

This caught the whole room by surprise and all looked at the professor with unbelieving eyes. The Professor turned away, his expression showing a curled lip and a sneer where a smile should be.

"The place in question is home to an illegal black market dealer of such antiquities. Your supplied description of this man and his car registration were most helpful, enabling us to put the final closure on many months of work."

"This is all ridiculous." objected Steven again, this time with a touch of embarrassment showing. "Why am I being subjected to this foolish hearsay ? I don't know whose idea this is, but I'm warning you now this had better cease. If this comes to me having my day in court you will all be sorry you started this inquisition."

Violet, still maintaining her poise, spoke softly:

"To finalize this presentation of facts, for clarity and the understanding of all present, I ask you Mr, Spencer, why did you bring Professor Tallman here to the Navajo council ?"

"That's a no brainer Mam. We are not the experts on Navajo antiquities. We are here for you to identify, not only the man, but also the artifacts in question. Can you help us on that ?"

Professor Tallman, speaking smugly now said,

"Of course they cannot help you on this. I am the trained, credentialed professional, not these home schooled farmers. Further more, these articles in so called question belong to me and me only and having such ownership entitles me to do what ever I want with my own property.

Agent Spencer was about to say something when Steven held up his hand, curtly remarking,

"I'm not finished. There is absolutely no way they can

identify these articles as they say there is. In case you people are forgetting, I also am a Navajo. I belong to the Navajo Nation. These are things I have collected over the years. These accusations on your part are absolutely false."

Whispering Wind stood and naturally all attention focused on him. Speaking only in the Navajo language, he addressed the professor. A quiet translation was provided by Lone Buffalo to the three agents.

"**D**igger of Bones." he said confidently, "You have not yet been accused of anything, but I am about to do so now."

"**D**o what you may old man, I have nothing to hide. You have no proof of anything that has been said so far."

Whispering Wind smiled and nodded   his head at Dove of Spring to continue for him.

"**T**he documents and articles we all speak of Professor Tallman, found in your possession upon your arrest belong here to the Navajo Nation. These documents are of great antiquity and go back thousands of years. Of course you knew that before you stole them. They were recently discovered here on our land by a Mr. Eric Dexter."

"**I** met this Mr. Dexter you speak of and he is not one of us. He is an outsider."

Whispering Wind interrupted quietly;

"**H**e is more Navajo then you Digger of Bones."

Tallman shot him a killing glance.

"**I**f what you say is true, where is this Mr. Dexter ?" the professor inquired smiling slyly. "Here you are falsely accusing me of misdeeds when perhaps this Mr. Dexter is the one you should be searching for. Where is this Dexter fellow I ask again ? Could it be that, if these documents do exist, as you claim, that he is the guilty one and confiscated your precious history and is now long gone. Where is your proof of my guilt."

Dove of Spring maintaining her calm demeanor answered quietly.

"**W**e will get to that soon enough Professor. In the meantime let me direct your attention to the box on the table. It contains photographic evidence from the time of discovery in situ. There is also photo coverage of the time they were brought here to the council room. Each document was then photographed individually in front of witnesses. This is our permanent record. The actual artifacts were under lock and key to be opened only for professional study by our people and experts for authentication. The key, it seems is missing and so are the priceless documents."

"That, in my opinion is poor proof of the accusations you have thrust upon me." huffed Steven authoritatively.

"I'm sure." continued Violet, "these gentlemen from the FBI will agree this is sufficient enough evidence to substantiate our claim. We have an actual photograph to match each and every artifact in your possession."

The professor sat up in his chair taking on his haughty air again.

"Well, instead of badgering me with these drummed up allegations, you should be out looking for this Dexter fellow. It appears to me he is the one missing along with your silly papers."

Each and every one of the elders showed great discomfort at hearing one of their own involved in such treachery. They all held questions but allowed Dove of Spring her time to outline the complete story.

"How do you know Mr. Dexter is missing. You have not been here for many days." questioned Violet.

"Well, er..,a-a-a.. It just stands to reason your papers are missing and he is not around. How long has he been gone ?

Steven Tallman then heard an all too familiar voice behind him.

"They don't have to go out and search for me professor. I've been here all the time."

Steven was now physically shaking. His face in a tight fearful expression. He managed to jump up from his seat and turned around. The two FBI agents on either side of him also stood each grabbing an arm to subdue him. Red faced he stuttered out,

"Yu, yu, you, you're a–al–." He stopped himself quickly.

Eric finished his sentence for him with a question mark.

"DEAD ? Is that what you were trying to say professor. That I'm dead."

Recovering quickly Tallman spit out;

"No, no. You're trying to put words in my mouth."

"Am I really now, Steven. You seem to have forgotten how you laughed as you pushed me down that deep, dark shaft, shoving dirt, rock and debris on top of me before slamming it closed knowing that I could not get out. Isn't that what you were going to say Steven. Go ahead, tell all these good people the true story of how you left me in the desert in a mine shaft, to die. Tell them how you then came back here saying I never met you at the pyramid. Then how you stole the key from Whispering Wind. The key that secured these ancient documents. And all this was for your personal financial gain. Wasn't it professor ?"

Whispering Wind stood drawing every ones attention.

"How many times have you done this before ? I did not want to believe it before today, but in the past, many sacred artifacts have disappeared and always around the time of your visits. The visits where you came home to be with your people. You have brought shame upon the Navajo. We the "Dineh" will recover. You shall now bear that burden the rest of your days."

The red faced professor was now perspiring profusely. The agents managed to reseat Tallman who was jabbering uncontrollably.

"This is all preposterous, this is all just hearsay. I don't even know who the man is. You are my people yet you let a stranger come to our homeland and fill you with all sorts of crazy ideas. You talk against one of your own."

Dove of Spring asserted herself once more.

"Do you have anything to say for yourself professor ?"

"I'm not going to dignify this circus act with another word" Steven mumbled

"I don't think anything more needs to be said." Agent Spencer put forth. Addressing the other two agents he added, :Take the good professor to the car and stay with him."

There was no struggle. Professor Steven Tallman left quietly, his head down.

Agent Spencer addressed the elders.

"There is no need for any further discussion. I will only take a short time more to validate the artifacts and photography. I do not think any further participation on your part will be necessary. I'm sorry you had to go through this. I do understand the value you put on your history.

Spencer joined Dan, myself and Violet at the far end of the table where we reviewed the photographic records along with the artifacts and actual documents. The whole story was told by a very animated Lone Buffalo. It covered from the time of discovery tracing its whole path up through being secured under lock and key. No more than twenty minutes had passed when Spencer stated he was more than convinced.

"Ordinarily we would hold this evidence until the trial was

over and the matter settled. But knowing what these things mean to you I think a duplicate copy of these photo's will suit our needs. You can forward them to my office. " he said as he handed me a business card.

All three of us signed depositions confirming the above discussion.

" If we ever need the real things we will contact you. That about wraps it up. We'll let you good people get back to your studies."

The agent shook our hands and Dan walked him out to the car leaving Violet and I alone.

"That went well for us." I said awkwardly.

"On the other hand," Violet smiled warmly gently touching my hand, "Thanks to you Hunter of Stories. You should have seen his face when he heard your voice. If that wasn't guilt then I don't know what is."

I did not move away from her touch nor did I answer it, and was relieved when Dan returned. We parted innocently as he barged through the door.

"Look what I have." he shouted holding up the special key to the chest.

We were both elated and could not wait to return it to Whispering Wind. The return of the key totally renewed my spirits.

"How about we celebrate tonight with a nice dinner and a good bottle of wine."

My remark generated big smiles from both.

"You two enjoy. I already have a previous commitment for dinner with my lady friend and her parents."

I think Violet's smile actually grew bigger upon hearing these words.

"Okay, my friend, your loss." I turned back to Violet. "Is that okay with you ?"

"That's fine ." rushed out of her mouth. "Perhaps we can make it a foursome another time."

"Sounds great to me." Dan answered.

We proceeded to clean up our messy table.

We all went our separate ways with my promise to pick up Dove of Spring at seven o'clock.

~ ~ ~ ~ ~ ~

"You're right on time. Funny, I kind of expected that of you" said Dove of Spring as she opened her door.

I stood there like a school boy staring at what was before me. Violet was not a beauty from a model magazine cover, but she did have that special handsome quality that only Native American women possess. Her hair, which had always been tied back, now hung freely to below her shoulders. The sheen of the raven black color picked up the highlights of any and all light reflection.

The dress was traditional soft deerskin adorned with multi colored beading accented by small turquoise stones of no special design. The neck of the dress was sort of a curved V just giving a hint of cleavage. The length fell a touch below the knee edged by the usual buckskin fringe. Soft leather boots highlighted her shapely calves. The overall beauty of her handsome face commanded the eyes attention. Her smile showed her perfect white teeth made even whiter by her lightly tanned flawless skin. I saw this woman of fifty for the first time as absolutely stunning.

I didn't know what to say and when I tried to speak the words wouldn't come out. I don't know how long I stood there. Her words finally registered with my vacationing brain.

"I thought we were going to dinner or are you just going to stand there all night."

My tongue at last connected with my head as I spurted out,

"You look positively lovely Violet. A perfect tribute to your name. Both of them."

Her smile was actually radiant now as she answered.

"Thank you kind sir. I did so want to impress you."

I offered her my hand as she stepped through the doorway. I held it until we got to my car. She made herself comfortable while I walked to the drivers side.

"I see you always bring your work with you." she said indicating the junk in the back seat."

I smiled in return stating I like to be prepared.

We made small talk as we drove and I found myself staring at her magnificent profile. She was truly a handsome woman.

Dinner with her was perfect. I had not felt this good or relaxed in a very long time. We chatted all evening about everything but us.

The ride home was definitely quiet, each not knowing where

to go from here. About ten minutes from the main compound on a lonely stretch of desert road we spotted a shooting star. I stopped the car and we were both quick to exit. It was more than just one shooting star. It appeared to be a meteor shower with each streak more breathtaking than the last. We oohed and aahhed for almost the whole eight or ten minute show. Each of us standing on our own side of the car. *"How stupid is this"* I yelled at myself quietly, nor did I make a move to change the situation.

The show ended and we finished our quiet ride home. I exited the parked car and walked to her side to open the door for her. I received a warm smile of thanks. Walking to her front door we continued our silence. We both stood there awkwardly not looking at each other like young teens. After a silent forever Violet half smiled and whispered;

"I had a lovely evening and I mean that sincerely."

She touched my hand and moved her head up to gently kiss my cheek.

"Thank you" she added as she moved away. "Good night." she whispered again.

I thought I detected moisture in her eyes as I turned and walked to the car. I was twenty five or so feet from her when I stopped and turned around. She was still standing there, bathed in the moonlight looking more radiant than earlier, if that was even possible. I walked back to her with one purpose in mind. When I reached her I enfolded her in my arms and kissed her as she deserved to be.

After many seconds we parted as I said softly,

"Good night Dove of Spring."

I turned and walked to the car without looking back. While I drove off she remained standing like a statue in the moonlight. I had not wanted to go that far, nor was I sorry I did. I drove back to the motel my mind totally confused.

My night was not what you would call restful. I did manage some sleep though it was not what I was used to. Oh how I missed my jungle serenade.

~ ~

I answered the phone, my head still in a fog.

"Hey sleepy head I thought we were going to close up your almost grave shaft today. " Dan's cheerful voice said.

I glanced at my watch reading nine twenty five. The time shocked me awake.

"**O**h, yeah, sure thing Dan." I replied. "I'll be there in an hour." I returned the phone to its cradle and headed for the shower. I was on my way in twenty minutes drinking my coffee as I drove.

~ ~

I joined Dan in the flatbed truck and into the desert we went.

"**H**ow did it go last night." he inquired.

"**F**ine." I answered in a non committal way. "You missed a good dinner."

Dan picked up on my discomfort and quickly changed the subject.

"**B**y the way I managed to get a small amount of gun powder. I thought we could use it to permanently close down your escape tunnel.

"**G**ood idea." I said enthusiastically. "We don't want to leave an open death trap."

I had not been back to the site since the night of my escape and obviously nothing had changed. Dan gassed up the backhoe and removed the covering to the shaft. Even though this was almost my final crypt I did not have a problem in descending to the bottom again. A more than thorough check of the walls and floor yielded no new hidden passages. Satisfied, I returned topside and Dan proceeded to fill the shaft with rock, gravel and sand. He even managed to break up the wooden platform and use it as fill in the hole. Available loose rocks along the sandstone wall were gathered as a final topping to the shaft. Mother nature would do the rest.

We then moved to my escape tunnel. Dan methodically set a few charges in various places and set off the light explosives. They more than adequately did their job. This also received a final topping with the backhoe and we were on our way home.

~ ~ ~ ~

"**D**oes this mean you're leaving us, or will you stay for a while longer ?" asked Lone Buffalo.

"**B**oth." was my strange reply.

Dan looked at me completely puzzled. I laughed at his expression and then explained.

"**T**here is nothing more I can do about the documents and

"The Book" or even the pyramid and it's museum. That is strictly your matter now. Or should I say the peoples concern, you know pursuing translations, verification, historical recordings. That, of course, I would like to hear results of, but that's easy enough to contact me."

Dan was looking for a more concrete answer which I could not give him because I didn't know myself..

"Where will you go and what will you do now ?"

"Well, for one thing I have yet to accomplish what I set out to do here."

"What was that ?"

"Ancient roads. Your ancient roads. You know the roads between your ancient ruins, or possibly locating new ruins."

"That's how you found the pyramid, wasn't it ?"

"It was." I replied. "But they were roads to nowhere."

"I wouldn't exactly agree with that." Dan smiled.

"Okay, so we lucked out on that, though I may still want to pursue looking for roads. If I had any sense at all I would go back home to Vermont and my business. I'm about out of money. Funny, that sounds even more serious when I say it out loud.

"You can always come back and search for the roads another time. I'll even help you if you want."

"I would hope you would. Tell you what I'll hang around a few more days before I shove off. I do want to revisit the pyramid at least once more. That place fascinates me so."

"Good." Dan blurted out happily. I will put myself at your disposal for your last few days. I must admit though I'll miss you."

"I'll miss this place also, especially all the excitement of discovery."

"I think you will be missed by others too." Dan said quietly.

We both knew who this was in reference to. I chose not to reply nor did he push any further.

We arrived back at the main compound where Dan let me out by the council room. He continued on to return the truck and backhoe to its garage.

"I'll see you later." he said with his usual cheerfulness.

Whispering Wind was in the council room looking at "The Book."

Without turning to look at me he spoke to me in our usual way.

"We are grateful, my young friend. You have returned our history to us which could have been lost forever. You are truly one of us. I now understand why your Mayan king chose you as a disciple. You are all peoples because you care. My thanks again Hunter of Stories.

I thanked him for his words, turning to leave. He followed with,

"Let not your other concern deter you from what you must do. She will always be here because her heart is also true. Talk to her. She will understand. Go my son. Continue your chosen work."

This man was utterly amazing. He can read into your very soul even when you have said nothing. I did feel better though because of his words. I found my car and returned to my motel.

I forced myself to spend the rest of the day catching up on my notes and journal entries. The journal I actually liked as I did in the jungle. I felt it validated myself in what I was doing.

I fixed a light supper and even thought about calling Violet but something inside of me said no. Around nine o'clock I grabbed a cold one and decided to sit out under the stars for a while. Just as I opened the door the phone rang. I set my beer down and picked up the phone.

"Dexter here."

"My aren't we formal tonight."

It was the soft sweet voice of Violet.

"I'm sorry." I replied. I had just put a call in back east, I thought this was my answer."

"You don't have to sound so disappointed that it's me." she chided.

I didn't answer that. Within a few seconds she continued;

"I missed you today. I was there twice but you had just left both times." There was a pause. I heard from Dan that you're planning to leave." she stated in a disappointed tone.

"Not for a few days." I answered matter of factly.

"You jerk Eric, why are you being so cold ?" I thought. With a softer voice I explained.

"**I** have a few more notes to finish up about our discoveries and I want to revisit the pyramid one last time."

"**O**h, I see." Was Violet's almost indifferent answer.

"**W**ould you care to join me ?" I asked in a soft gentle tone.

"Now that was more like it" I told myself.

"**A**re you sure about that." she questioned back.

Without hesitation I answered "Yes, I'm very sure."

There was no hesitation on her part either.

"**W**hat time would you like me to be ready ?"

Suppose I pick you up around ten. Is that okay ?"

"**O**f course. If you want to make it earlier that would be okay also."

"**N**o let's keep it at ten. I have some errands to take care of first."

"**T**hat will be just fine, Eric. I look forward to tomorrow. And Eric ?"

"**Y**es ?"

"**T**hank you." she whispered ever so quietly, followed by "Good night."

Then I heard a click as she hung up the phone. I sat there a moment holding the receiver until the dial tone sounded.

"**L**et's hope you're right Whispering Wind." I mumbled to no one.

I reached for my not so cold beer and headed outside. The night was cool, the stars painted the sky while the breeze sang softly over the sands, interrupted now and then by the haunting cry of a coyote. My jungle came to mind and I could feel myself surrendering to its mystic music.

The singing tires of a truck whizzing by awakened me. It was two twenty in the morning. I returned to the room and bed after setting the alarm just in case.

~

I didn't need the alarm. I guess I was more anxious than I thought. Leaving my rooms just before nine, remembering a small pet shop near the library, I headed in that direction. The shop, as small as it appeared, was ideal and had a decent supply of what I wanted. I chose a few each of crickets, grasshoppers and June beetles. The attendant packed them nicely in a box with plenty of air holes.

I was on my way again already thinking of Dove of Spring. Part of me did harbor a strong attraction for her. A more common sense part of me, because of my adventurous cravings, pushed me away from any long term commitments. I would hope to keep Violet as a friend but beyond that I truly wanted my freedom. I felt she already had a hint of this, and perhaps today my intentions would be clarified and not in my usual cold manner.

I neared her home and was getting that school boy feeling looking forward to seeing her. She was out the door as I pulled up to the curb. Like the other night she was adorned with the traditional buckskin highlighted with bead work and turquoise. Instead of the skirt she was wearing leggings, fringe down both outside legs. The raven hair still hung to her shoulders picking up the glancing rays of the early sun. She posed a vision even I found hard to resist.

Before I exited the car she was there opening the door herself. Once settled she smiled saying;

"I am so grateful for this opportunity. Thank you for your willingness to drag me along. I also wanted to see your pyramid in detail and not in an official capacity."

"I'm glad you're here. I would like sharing my passion of discovery with you."

I took off to the desert and we did the usual small talk, the weather and so on. She asked directly as if asking permission,

"Can I meet your famous Mr. Blue ?"

I quickly gazed at her. She was shyly smiling.

"I hope we do see him. I can't answer for him but I'm sure he would be pleased to meet such a lovely lady."

"Thank you kind sir. " she beamed.

It was obvious we were both comfortable now. I hoped it could stay that way.

Violet was like a child when we arrived at the pyramid. She wanted to see everything in all its detail. That's when I found out she had an engineering background. In fact she graduated from M I T. Yet again I was amazed by this remarkable woman.

She studied the structure as if she were still a student. I was pleased to tell her the story of how we discovered it. She soaked up every detail with genuine interest. I kicked on the generator as we entered the darkness. Now with light a plenty we stepped onto the make shift elevator and roped our way down. Our first stop was the turquoise room. We spoke respectfully of the imprisoned dead miners. I thanked her and the elders a second time for allowing such a caring service and burial.

She was also taken by the method used to adhere the turquoise stone to the false platform hiding the stairwell to the museum room. That soon passed because she was interested in moving to the room below as was I. She stood at the entrance for a long moment taking it all in.

"**I** can't believe the history we are seeing." she murmured.

We each went a different pathway closely viewing each and every artifact where it lay. Violet particularly admired and compared a soft deerskin dress with her own attire of today's world. Holding the dress up to show me she beamed with pride.

"**N**ow this is what I call tradition. There was but little change over the centuries."

I felt and understood her pride. I redirected Violets attention to the mural which captivated her as it did me. She studied every detail while I told her of the story of the mural hallway back in the Yucatan and how this mural carried the same style as if done by the same artist. She appeared excited by every word I uttered. I further went on about Diego and his commission by the king to depict our arrival at the lost city while she continued to gaze at the mural.

I was drawn to the Maya apparel which gave me a feeling of familiarity. My mind drifted to the lost city wondering what progress the team was making. I was still spellbound by the scrolls, waiting for their translated message and whether today's world was ready for it. I almost wished I had gone with them, but I would have been of little help since linguistics was not my forte'.

I must have really drifted into my jungle world because I suddenly realized someone was calling my name. Dove of Spring was by my side lightly touching my arm.

"**C**ome back to me Eric." were her delicately spoken words.

Embarrassed, I looked into her dark eyes whispering,

"**I**'m sorry."

"**I**t's alright Eric. I know you were where you really want to be. And that is not here. I totally understand."

She took both my hands in hers with a gentle pressure and smiled.

"It's okay that you leave, my love. I had you for a brief moment and I'll cherish that always. I'll not hold you back from your true love, jungle adventure. Your journal exposed your whole soul and who you truly are. You already have and always will inspire others. That's the real man I fell in love with and because I love you I will let you go."

There was a slight pause until she added,

"But not this very moment." she grinned. "We must finish this final inspection of this priceless history." her arms indicating the whole room. "And by the way, I know you didn't notice but I brought along a small picnic lunch for us so we don't have to rush back home."

She was as happy as a schoolgirl now and I must admit I felt that a burden, self-induced though it was, had been lifted from my whole being.

I walked to her and put my arms around her, her head on my shoulder. I held her tightly for a moment till she broke from my embrace. She smiled.

"Enough of that, we have work to do and besides I still have yet to meet your famous tarantula."

I laughed with her feeling very good about the whole togetherness thing.

We finished our detailed scrutiny of the museum and went out to the fresh air. Violet retrieved the lunch goodies from the car while I gathered my pet shop purchase.

"You brought lunch also ?" she inquired.

"Not exactly." I replied. "At least not for us."

She looked at me, question marks showing in her eyes.

"I'll explain in a while.

We covered the hot sand with an old canvas tarp I had in the car and sat down.

"Lunch is not much, just a quick sandwich and some lemonade." she smiled.

"At least you remembered, I totally forgot which is usual for me." I laughed back.

We quietly munched for a few minutes when I noticed Violet

staring past me.

"**W**ell, Mr. Blue. I finally get to meet you. It is my pleasure. I also want to thank you for helping my friend Eric. What you did meant a lot to a great many people."

By the time she finished her greeting she was beaming that wonderful smile. Turning to Mr. Blue I smiled also.

"**H**ello Pal, the lady who just introduced herself is a very special friend. Her name is Violet."

Grinning back to her contagious smile,

"**I** don't even feel embarrassed anymore for talking to my blue friend."

"**Y**ou shouldn't." offered Violet, "He did save your life which made me extremely happy."

Mr. Blue moved closer as if anticipating something. Remembering my pet shop bag I said;

"**O**kay my friend, I promised you something special and I'm keeping that promise."

Opening the box I dumped out a grasshopper and a cricket. Violet and I watched as he struck like lightening and immobilized them both. I followed with the other critters only to see his repeat performance.

"**N**ow my friend, enjoy and thank you.

While I watched Mr. Blue move toward the pyramid dragging a grasshopper I felt the warm presence of Dove of Spring next to me as she kissed my cheek.

"**Y**ou're such a warm thoughtful and giving man. Who could not like you?   She moved away while my cheeks burned red with embarrassment. Violet changed back to her normal tone.

"**H**e is a beautiful creature. I'm happy the Great Spirit introduced you two."

We enjoyed our lunch over the next hour while watching Mr. Blue making trips back and forth to the pyramid with his new found treasures. As silly as it sounds we marveled at his efforts at caching his unexpected food supply. When all was put away Mr. Blue returned stopping about four feet away from me. He stared at me for a moment which I took as thanks.

"**Y**ou're welcome." I responded aloud.

I saw a leg twitch then he slowly turned away in no particular hurry.

"**Y**ou are amazing." I heard Violet say. She was wearing a proud smile for me. I selfconsciously smiled back not knowing what to say.

The awkward moment passed and Violet made another close inspection of the pyramids construction. Another hour or so passed, my notes finished, we agreed to head home.

Violet spoke as soon as the car moved.

"**T**hank you again, Eric for the day. It meant a lot to me. We the people have so much to thank you for. The "Dineh" will always be in your debt."

I could feel the red blush of embarrassment building.

"**I** did nothing special and no thanks are necessary. It was something I got pleasure and a sense of accomplishment from." I answered humbly.

She sensed my shyness and changed the subject.

"**I** want to ask you a question and I want you to be truly honest with me. Please."

"**I** promise."

"**W**ould you consider a home cooked meal with me this evening? If you think that would make you uncomfortable to be alone with me then perhaps we can ask Dan and his lady friend to join us."

Boy, her straight forwardness hit me like a hammer, yet I know there was no malice in her words. I did not want to hesitate too long so I replied as fast as my brain would allow and as warm as I could.

"**I** would love to have dinner with you tonight and alone would be my preference."

I glanced at her as I finished speaking only to see her eyes wishfully looking back at me. Then came the warm, truly loving smile. It felt good to make her happy.

We chatted more about what I did in the lost city and I also learned more of her background. It was her choice to stay with her people as opposed to the hectic outside business world. She felt her contributions were more appreciated. This I could not disagree with.

We arrived at her house and walked unashamedly hand in hand to the door. The house was small but warmly appointed with tradition intermingling with some of today's modern conveniences.

"**P**lease, make yourself comfortable while I fix us some dinner."

"**W**hat can I do to help ?"

"**A**bsolutely nothing." she answered with a kiss to my forehead. "Allow me the pleasure of spoiling you. It will be my only chance to do so."

Again she spoke with that winning smile and absolutely no malice what so ever knowing the situation between us. I suddenly recognized how long it had been since someone loved me like this, and yet I did not want any restrictions on my freedom.

Violet went ahead with dinner preparations cheerfully as she moved about.

"**W**e're almost ready Eric, if you would care to open the wine. Dinner was a simple fare of meat loaf with mushroom gravy and assorted veggies. It was amazingly delicious with a distinct flavor which I found out later was a beef and buffalo combination.

After dinner we sat out under the stars listening to soft mood music of her choice. I guess the atmosphere of dinner and wine caught up to me when I took her in my arms and kissed her not wanting to stop. With a gentle pressure she pushed me away.

"**N**o, Eric, let's not spoil a perfect evening or an even more perfect relationship. I'll always be here for whenever you think you're ready to continue."

I knew she was right. I attempted to apologize but was hushed with her finger to my lips.

"**E**njoy this night so you have something to remember." she smiled with a quick kiss to my cheek.

"**I** guess I should go." I said quietly.

"**N**o, not just yet." she answered holding my hand.

We walked hand in hand for more than an hour with a gentle squeeze every now and then to let each other know of our feeling. Circling to my car we said a final good night. I drove away looking in the rear view mirror at her bathed in the moonlight. It had been both a happy and sad night which led to a very restless sleep. I don't know what the right answer was nor did I know if I ever would.

Chapter 23

I did not see Violet or talk to her the next day, nor did either of us call. I was more than busy getting ready to leave these wonderful people. Dan and I reviewed a lot of things relating to our discoveries.

Even the school kids held a fare well lunch for me. Whispering Wind had summoned me after the surprise luncheon. I gave my thanks to the teens for their thoughtfulness and walked to the elders hogan. As was his habit he bid me enter before I got there. He greeted me with a cool lemonade indicating I sit across from him away from the fire.

"Hunter of Stories you have done yourself proud. We the people are grateful for what you have provided us. These missing pieces of our history will keep our young ones with us so that we shall carry our name forward as we have carried it from the past. Nothing is really new or old. It is only that time passed between the two."

Whispering Wind paused allowing me to digest his words which was not hard to do. Everything he said made sense to me. I knew he was reading my mind by the way he continued.

"I feel that you have finally settled the matter of the heart. She will be here for you but you always knew that. She will be of great assistance to you in the future. Do not let that escape you. Listen to the words of your Mayan king. Go, do the work you must and return to us. As I have spoken earlier, you are true Navajo as you are Mayan, as you will be all peoples."

I stood to leave. Whispering Wind approached me putting one hand on my head with the other touching my heart.

-The Ancient Ones-

"These two and the Great Spirit will guide you always. Our final farewell will be in the morning. You will go now."

I made my way back to Dan's office trying to figure out how he knew I wasn't leaving until the next morning.

Dan and I joked about going to the lost city together, but down deep inside I believe we were both serious. We finally parted knowing I would be here in the morning for a final good bye.

My night was uneventful, filled with final packing and settling my bill for the rooms. I made a snack for dinner and lay down for a night of uninterrupted sleep.

~ ~ ~ ~

I arrived at the compound at nine AM and parked where Dan was waiting for me. Surprisingly the place appeared almost deserted. Not even a barking dog was to be heard. Dan, both happy and sad, greeted me with a firm and sincere handshake. Then with his usual smile said,

"I have been instructed to escort you to the council fire." I was a bit confused but walked with him. We entered the hogan to a full house. Once I was seated, Sky Above the Mountain performed his fire ritual and blessing. The chant and drums stopped as Whispering Wind stood uttering in Navajo. Dove of Spring also arose and walked to me. Dan urged me to stand as she neared me. Being as official as she could but still with her loving smile, she spoke;

"On behalf of the Navajo Nation, Whispering Wind and the elders wished me to give this to you." She handed me one of the scrolls we had discovered. "Share this with your Mayan friends. Once it's meaning is known we hope you will share it with us as we will share the interpretations of the others with you. You have the best wishes of our nation and The Great Spirit. Go and fulfill your destiny."

Looking straight into my eyes she whispered, "Return to me."

She turned and walked to her place with the elders.

I stuttered at a total loss for words, finally;

"I am deeply honored by your words and trust. I will do all in my power to live up to that trust, and yes I do believe that I am part of you and proud to be so."

I could feel a bit of moisture building in my eyes, and actual tears once they started applauding. Dan led me outside. We stood by the entranceway as each and every person in attendance passed and wished me a good journey and either shook my hand or touched my shoulder. The elders were the last to depart but they also repeated the same routine.

Whispering Wind and Dove of Spring were the very last. Whispering Wind touched my heart and nodded knowing I understood.

Dove of Spring put her arms around me and kissed me like a lover for all to see. After a very long moment she broke the embrace and without a word walked away. She did not look back.

Whispering Wind smiled and nodded again quietly saying.

"She will always be here."

When I came out of my trance like state all was quiet and I was alone save for my ever smiling friend, Dan.

"Come on Pal, I'll walk you to your car."

The End

References

1- America's Ancient Civilizations
by A. Hyatt & Ruth Verrill
Pub. By G.P.Putnam & Sons, N.Y.

2- In Search of Ancient North America
by Heather Pringle
Pub. By John Wiley & Sons Inc.

3- Touch the Earth
by T.C. Mclunan
Pub. By OuterBridge & Lazord, Unc.

4- Daily Life in Pre-Columbian Native America
by Clarissa W. Confer
Pub. By Greenwood Press

5- The Enduring Navajo
by Laura Gilpin
Pub. By University of Texas Press.

6- The Navajo's
by John Upton Terrell
Pub by Weybright & Talley

7- Aztecs of Mexaco
by George C. Vaillant
Pub by Doubleday & Company, Inc.

8- The Ancient Sun Kingdom's of the America's
by Alberto Beltran
Pub. By The World Publishing Co.

9- The Smithsonian   (April 2016)
"Invisible Kingdom"
By Joshua Harper
10- The Map That Changed the World.
By Simon Winchester
Pub by Harper Collins Publishers

11- Maps of the Ancient Sea Kings
by Charles H. Hapgood
Pub by Adventures Unlimited Press

12- The Navajo
by James F. Downs
Pub by Holt, Rinehart and Winston, Inc.

13- Lost Knowledge of the Ancients
by a Graham Hancock Reader
Pub by Bear & Company

14- Ancient Mines of Kitchi - Gummi
by Roger Jewell
Pub by Jewell Histories

15- Who Discovered America
by Gavin Menzies & Ian Hudson
Pub by William Morrow

~ ~ ~ ~ ~ ~